AMERICA AWAITS US, MY LOVELY
AND OTHER STORIES

AMERICA AWAITS US, MY LOVELY

AND OTHER STORIES

Christopher Owen

Matador
9 Priory Business Park,
Wistow Road, Kibworth Beauchamp,
Leicestershire. LE8 0RX
Tel: 0116 279 2299
Email: books@troubador.co.uk
Web: www.troubador.co.uk/matador
Twitter: @matadorbooks

ISBN 978 1838595 487

British Library Cataloguing in Publication Data.
A catalogue record for this book is available from the British Library.

Printed and bound in the UK by TJ Books Ltd, Padstow, Cornwall
Typeset in 11pt Minion Pro by Troubador Publishing Ltd, Leicester, UK

Matador is an imprint of Troubador Publishing Ltd

CONTENTS

AMERICA AWAITS US,
MY LOVELY

London. 1960. Irene Walker, eighty-three years old, is seated in her armchair by the living-room window in her flat in North London. It is eleven in the morning. Eddie, her husband, is out, gone to put a bet on.

She married Eddie when she was seventy-nine years old. At the time, she declared she had been a widow for fifty years and that she and Eddie would be company for each other in their dotage. Her decision had met with no small measure of resistance from her grown-up children, Helen, Frances and Walter.

'I'm not discussing the matter,' she had said to them.

She has in her lap a solicitor's letter she has received this morning. She puts it on the table at her side. Picks it up again, puts it back in her lap. She leans back in her chair.

1903. Birmingham. The people struggling, making do. Children by the thousands shipped to strange lands, to Canada, Australia, South Africa. The unemployed. The charity breadlines.

'This is no country for the living,' Alec had said. 'Heigh-ho and heave-ho, we're off, my lads, for an adventure of a lifetime,' he had said before he set out from Liverpool to sail to New York City, to stay with his friend Albert Fitton in Buffalo. 'We'll be all right with him,' he had said to Irene.

Full of boldness, he was. She couldn't help but fall for him, be taken up by his charm, his optimism.

'My friend Albert, we'll be all right with him,' Alec wrote to her all those years ago. 'You'll be joining me out here in New York. So, pack up what you can but not too much, for there's opportunity over here and no arguing.'

He was a Birmingham man, of rough and ready stock, she couldn't deny that.

'Buy yourself the ticket,' Alec had said to her. 'I'm here waiting for you.'

Birmingham, the city of a thousand trades, that's what they used to say, engineering, metal, cutlery, nails and screws, guns, tools – tools were the thing, and wasn't Alec a tool-maker and hadn't he come up with tools to manufacture tin cans, and weren't there – 'for God's sake, won't you listen?' he had said to Irene – weren't there, he said, huge markets, vast opportunities for the can-making tools in parts of Canada and the United States where they grew the fruit, the peaches, the cherries and plums.

'You've got to get in there early, my lovely, before the other buggers clean up,' he said. 'Before some other bastard steals the patent, mocks up an inferior version, flogs it, undercuts the price. God help us, one can't be sitting on one's arse doing naught. One has to go, go, get out there and make a living, conquer the world,' he said to her. He said it out loud, voice raised, he let all of them know, there in the Red Lion when he was three parts gone with the beer. He was fond of his beer. 'Too fond,' her father said.

'America awaits us, my lovely,' Alec wrote from New York where he had gone to make the contacts, to prepare the ground. 'The world is our oyster. Just have to find the way to prise it open and take up the pearl.'

'Lady Intrepid' he had once called her. She was up for a challenge, he said. He could use words, this mechanic. He was a classy act. He could put on the style. He could smile. That smile was his passport. She always thought that. It was his guarantee.

'We'll get married the day you arrive, the very day, my lovely Irene. I've made the arrangements, it's all in hand.'

It comes back to her in her old age now. There she was, twenty-six years old, due to sail on the SS Lucania from Liverpool, to arrive at the port of New York City after seven days.

And there she was, filling in the Emigration Form. She remembers every detail of it. It comes back to her now unbidden. She can't remember what she had for her tea last night but she can remember the Emigration Form. *Gender?* Female. *Marital status?* Single. *Occupation?* Cashier. (At the Albion Lamp Company, Aston Road, North Birmingham. She was there with Betty and Doris and Marcia, all young women they were together – all of them gone now.) *Able to read and write?* Yes. *Nationality?* British. *Race?* English. *Residence?* Birmingham. *Final destination?* New York. *Ticket?* Yes. Paid by self. $50.

'Fifty dollars, it's only fifty dollars,' Alec wrote. 'I've not got it on me just yet, with the expenses over here, but you can borrow it from Eric or one of your other brothers, Eric's OK for a bit, for a loan, tell him I'll pay it back soon as soon, he can rely on it, no trouble.'

The Emigration Form had asked if she had been to the States

before. No, she had written. Who was she going to join? My future husband Alec P. Bowker. 97 Barrow Street, New York.

'We'll be staying there for a few days, have a look around Manhattan,' Alec had written. Then they'd be staying with his friend Albert Fitton. Albert Fitton had gone out and married a Polish American girl.

Irene in her armchair in West London puts the solicitor's letter back on the table at her side, picks up the passenger logbook which she had recently rediscovered in a box at the back of the hall cupboard. She reads that SS Luciana was a British passenger ship built in 1893 by Fairfield Govan for the Cunard Steamship Company. The print is faded – it looks as if something has been spilt on it – and her cataracts don't help – she makes out... *the first-class public room... staterooms... upper deck... oak... thickly carpeted... first-class dining...white and gold... Ionic pillars... panel... pilasters and decoration.* Alec had made a point of remarking upon the luxury. It was as if the ship was his, that he owned it. That was Alec, that's how he was. He would have her enjoy the opulence of it all. Only, of course, she was travelling second class.

'Don't you worry, my darling,' he had written to her. 'It may be second class this time around, but, mark my words, my lovely, in a few years' time, in no time whatever, it'll be you and me in first class intermingling with the toffs, ordering the champagne, feeling up the velvets.'

There was a woman on board. She was called Jane Devonshire or Devonport. She said she was from Cambridge, Massachusetts. She'd been to England to see her brother. There was that woman in her furs from Darlington with her two boys who was joining her husband in Boston. Mrs Charter, that was her name. Irene's not thought of her, not since the voyage out. But there she is now in her furs.

Irene, her old legs painful from the arthritis, pulls herself out of her armchair, goes to the drinks' cabinet with its glass front. It's a quarter past eleven.

'Barrow Street in West Village was a shock,' she says to herself as she pours a Martini. 'Those narrow streets, rubbish everywhere. So many Africans.'

'We'll not be here for long,' he had said.

She unsteadily makes her way back to her chair. She sits, settles herself. She sips her Martini.

There he was, waiting for her, as he'd promised, and he took her in his arms and lifted her in the air.

'Quick. We've got to make an honest woman of you,' he said, and off they went to the marriage-licence place.

And then – and then – he took her on a whirlwind tour of Manhattan, he did. He showed her with pride and excitement the Statue of Liberty as if it was his own. Then there was Central Park, there was, and the flower market in Union Square, the Grand Army Plaza. And they took a trip to Coney Island and paddled in the sea. They were on their honeymoon, he said, and well they might be, she thought, it costing him as it did.

'You wait,' he said to her. 'You wait – in the next few years this place will be transformed, it will be unrecognisable.'

They were standing on Broadway, in Times Square. They were stepping out on Brooklyn Bridge which could not fail to impress. They walked the length of it into Brooklyn and back again and landed up at the Assonia Hotel, where they had tea. The Assonia had air-conditioning, Alec told her. He told her all proud as if he'd put it in himself. She had never been in such a grand place. He had bought himself a new suit for twenty-five dollars. He stood there in his suit, brown with a white fleck. New brown leather shoes.

'One has to look one's best, my lovely,' he said to her. 'You've got to impress. People out here don't buy unless you look good, like you don't need to sell. Then they buy,' he said. 'We're off to my friend Albert in Buffalo,' he said.

She can't remember Albert Fitton – can't put a face to him or his wife. They'd stay with Albert, he said, while he did the business in New York and then they'd be off to Pennsylvania. There was a man there. He owned thousands of acres in the Lake Erie fruit and vegetable belt. He was looking to invest in tin-making machinery. Alec was onto a winner, he was sure of that. And that, he said, would only be the start of things.

'Buffalo is the eighth largest city in the United States and the largest grain-milling centre in the country,' she remembers him proudly telling her the first day they were there.

He showed her the Ellicott Square Building which cost $3.5 million to build, he said. It was built in under one year and Buffalo was the first city in the United States to have electric street lighting. Alec knew it all.

'America is only just starting,' he said.

He pointed out a car – they were in Main Street. It was called – what was it called? – it was called the Arrow, made by the Pierce Arrow Motor Car Company. She can see it now. She doesn't have to close her eyes. It was red, sleek, leather interior.

'One day,' he said, 'we'll be driving around in one of those. You don't come to America unless you think big.'

They were going to Pennsylvania, he said.

She had Helen in the hospital in Franklin. Took fourteen hours. 'You've a reluctant child in there,' one of the doctors said.

Alec wasn't there. Men not permitted. When he came in after the baby was born, he smelt of beer. You couldn't blame him. Fourteen hours of waiting.

'Our first child,' he announced. He was excited, he was enthusiastic. He always was.

'How did the business meeting go?' she asked him there in the hospital.

'Fine, fine. Putting the last bits and pieces of the contract together,' he said.

'Will we be rich?'

'Not as rich as I'd like,' he said. 'There's a lot of competition. But, fingers crossed, old girl, it'll keep us going. The man's bought non-exclusive usage and all that.'

She didn't really understand. She can hear his voice, the way he talked then. The bravado.

'We'll have a few more weeks, we'll get you and Helen well and on-your-feet, then we'll take a trip on Lake Erie. I've always wanted to go on Lake Erie. We'll have a great time,' he said.

'We're off to Canada,' he said. 'We'll be staying in Barton. Rented accommodation. There's great demand for cans in Canada – peaches, plums, cherries, all sorts. You go where the business takes you,' he said.

In Canada, she had Frances, a sister for Helen. After Canada it was back to Pennsylvania where she had Walter. Then in 1910 – she remembers the year, it comes to her clearly – she can't remember the name of her next-door neighbour half the time but she remembers the year, 1910 – back they came to Canada, mid-winter, to Barton in Wentworth, Ontario. Yes, and it was there she had Robert, seven pounds eight ounces. Four children. Four mouths to feed. With the temperature at minus 36 degrees Fahrenheit, the children's bodies rubbed all over with goose grease, sewn into their long woollen underclothes to keep out the cold, the freezing rain and snow. Alec digging out the snow from the sidewalk, bringing in the firewood.

Then it'd been Orrtanna in Adams County, the canning factories of Biglerville and Gardners. The orchards. The peaches, the cherry, the apples. The sunrises.

'We've got to see Gettysburg,' Alec said.

And the blossom everywhere.

'We could farm here,' he says. 'We could farm here.'

Only we can't. But it doesn't stop him saying it.

He hadn't been home for six days.

'I've met someone else,' he said. He'd fallen in love, he told her, and he'd come home to collect his things. She'd seen the girl. She couldn't have been more than eighteen, if that. Blonde hair, standing there with him, she looking up at him, he all on show. She entranced, no doubt. The silly little bitch. What did she think she was up to? The two of them coming out of Maple Leaf Park. She can't remember her name. He told her it was best she and the children went back to England, to her mother and brothers. He said he'd send her money. But he didn't.

Back home in Aston she told everyone that Alec was dead. She was a widow, she said. To be sent home by her husband, that was too great a shame. It was a disgrace.

Irene is seated in her armchair. Her hand goes out to the solicitor's letter on the side table. She re-reads it. It's telling her that Alec died four weeks ago. On the 4th of August 1960. Alec's dead. And he's been alive all these years. She'll not tell Helen, Frances and Walter. She'll not tell Eddie. Why upset the poor man? There's nothing anyone can do about it, she tells herself. The solicitor's letter says Alec P. Bowker had been living in England, in Farnham, Hampshire, since 1926. Her address was among his possessions. He'd come back and not told her. He found out where she was but he'd made no effort to see her or the children, and he, the self-centred fool was there – doing what? – in Hampshire. The girl had given him his marching orders, she'd not be surprised, and no wonder. A seventeen-year old, no older than nineteen, that was for sure, him out there with his grand ideas, his foolishness. There were his offspring, his and hers, and off he went, the useless fool, the callous oaf. She had loved this man. Those early years, the adventure, his promises. She's never forgotten him. He's been with her ever since. And he's died of pneumonia at the age of eighty-seven, the letter says.

Irene hears the front door open. It's Eddie.

'It's me,' she hears him call.

Irene takes the letter and slips it behind the cushion at her back. Eddie is there. In the doorway.

STORE SECURITY

None too bright in the head, that's what they said of him, that's what he thought they said, him standing there in the supermarket, on one foot and then the other. Store security, that's him. Mondays to Fridays 8.30 a.m. till 5.30 p.m. Keep an eye open for shoplifters, the manager had said. Although he'd not seen any, any evidence of any, in all the two years he'd been turning up for work five days a week. Got a job though, his old dad says. Got a job, lad – him calling him lad, and him forty-three. Count your blessings, lad, his dad says. You're fortunate. In my day... in my day... off he goes, his dad – got a job though. Only it's nothing to shout about. Standing on one foot and then the other, watching the customers load their trolleys, select their purchases, load their trolleys.

The woman with the beret, the red and blue scarf, the watery eyes, it's baked beans every time. Comes in twice a week, it's baked beans, it's Cyprus potatoes, courgettes, the bananas, the not quite ripe bananas in the cellophane wrapping, the smaller ones. Takes her time choosing. Time on her hands, that's what he reckons. Picks up one bunch, puts it back, then another, looks at it, intently at it, puts it back, picks up the first she picked up, puts it down. Same with the courgettes – he himself doesn't eat courgettes, never has – it's the same with them. They look all alike to him. What's she going to do with a courgette? he says to young Tim stacking shelves. You wouldn't want to know, young Tim says, and bursts into laughing. All morning, every time he sees him, bursts into laughing.

Jenny works Tuesdays to Thursdays. She always has a cheery word. A big smile. How are you, John? she asks. Every time. All right. I'm all right, he says to her. That's the job, she says. Keep the flag flying, she says. Keep the flag flying, he says to her, calls over when she passes, when he takes a walk up and down the fruit and veg aisle, comes across her stacking shelves. Keep the flag flying, he says over to her, her back to him as she stacks, stretches up or bends down to 'refresh the stock.' She's refreshing the stock, young Tim calls over, and laughs. He likes to laugh, does Tim, that's for sure, no doubt about it. John can't think why he laughs, has to laugh, the way he's always laughing. Keeps him going, John supposes. Jenny's married. He overheard her tell the Pole who works Tuesdays and Thursdays. I'm married, she told him. I'm married, thank you, she said to him. John heard her say it. I'm a married woman, thank you very much, she said.

John's place is among the shelves, in the aisles. Start the one end of the aisle, he was instructed when he first started, keep your eyes open. Keep your distance, John, don't impose yourself on the customer, don't intrude yourself, John. Then change your position, walk up and down the aisles from time to time, he was told. Keep your eyes open. Nothing doing, he tells his old dad. Nobody tries to steal nothing without paying, he says. That's because you're there keeping your eyes skinned, his dad says. If you weren't there, they'd be at it, getting away with murder, his dad says. You're holding down a responsible position, John, he says. Be proud. Not everyone has a job, not a job like what you got, John. Keep the flag flying, dad, John says. What's that? his dad says. Keep the flag flying, John says.

On one foot and then the other. Keeping criminality at bay. Jenny, Tuesdays, Wednesdays, Thursdays. The courgette customer is here, making herself a deep study of the bananas. Young Tim is cheerful, whenever was he not? The mid-afternoon young women with their kids, little kids. They're middle-class, them who come in there, his dad says. Young women with their little kids, well behaved, little boys and girls in good clothes. There's the old man with the stick, one foot after another, stopping now and then, every few feet, with his wire basket, two apples, two bananas, a ready-meal at the ready-meal shelves. They say he's famous, Tim tells him and laughs. An intellectual. A professor. Seen him on television. Archaeology. Roman remains. An international authority. Look at him, waiting to move again, mustering the resolve, the impulse to arrive at the ready-steady-go meals. Jenny helps him. John would go and help him himself, but he's not supposed to fraternise with the customers, has to keep his distance, he was told. The professor is known here, in the supermarket. He passes by. Stops. Walks on, his mind on Roman remains, bygone history, his books, his lectures, his hesitant, studied seeking out of the ready-steady-go meals, and Jenny at his elbow, one step forward, then another, Jenny's arm in his, like they're married. I'm a married woman, thank you very much, she told the Pole.

The courgette woman is in again. Must be Thursday. She's selecting the courgettes, one by one, pack by pack. It'll be the bananas next. You like courgettes, he says to her. She looks up at him, her eyes are watery. She doesn't seem to understand. Them courgettes, he says, you always buying them. You got to like them.

I don't eat them myself, he says. The woman says something he can't understand. She's foreign, he tells Tim who goes off laughing. She's foreign, he says to Jenny at the apples. Oh, she says and stacks the shelf with the apples. She's foreign, he tells his dad. The courgette woman, I speak to her about the courgettes, she's foreign, she doesn't speak English, he says. You don't want to speak to the customers, John, Dad says, foreign or otherwise, that's not your job, John. Store security, that's what you are, John.

Next time she's in, the foreign courgette woman, she smiles at him, a small smile. A smile definitely, without showing her teeth. He doesn't know what to do about that. He wonders if he ought to say something about it to Jenny, to Tim, only he doesn't want to make a mountain out of it, doesn't want to bring attention to himself in relation to a customer, foreign or otherwise. Next time she's in, he nods, he nods but she doesn't respond, so he's lost the chance, the opportunity, he tells himself. He had an opportunity and he's lost it, cos when she smiled just that bit, he hadn't said anything or smiled back or acknowledged the smile, her smiling, so she'd given up on him. He was back where he started.

When she's in next, John thinks he'll have a word, then as he is about to do so, he sees the manager looking in his direction, so he doesn't. He doesn't say anything. He'd like to, but he doesn't. He was going to say something to her, he says to his dad back home, but then he sees the manager looking. You don't want to say nothing to the customer, Dad says. You're store security, John, he says.

The following week, she's there again at the bananas. She looks up and sees him. Keep the flag flying, he says to her.

LIFE'S A BITCH

He had this dog, golden retriever, took it with him everywhere. He called her Bomber. He took it into pubs, the ones he frequented across the Midlands and in the North West. In he'd go, into the pub, the dog leading the way.

'Come on, Bomber. In you go,' he'd call out as he entered the bar, and faces would turn, customers look up and see the dog entering, then see Derek himself. The dog would hurry in, her tail wagging, making a lot of the moment and of the customers, who of course knew her and knew Derek, her owner.

'How do, Bomber,' they'd say.

'Alright, Derek,' they'd say.

Derek would call out brusquely, 'Come here, you silly dog. Come here,' as the dog moved excitedly in and about the customers' legs at the bar and sometimes at the neighbouring tables.

Not that anyone ever objected. But Derek called to her just the same, for it was his way, and it was the way he knew to start up a conversation and induce a feeling of camaraderie into the occasion. That was Derek's way. Bomber was an asset.

'Come over here, you silly dog,' he'd call.

'Sit, Sit,' he'd command, and eventually the dog would sit, and Derek would order his drink.

'A pint of your very best, if you please, guv'nor,' he'd call out in a voice louder than might be thought necessary, and he'd turn to those on his right or his left, and announce: 'Cor, bloody nippy tonight, isn't it?' and those on his right or left would agree that it was, though it was going to be wet at the weekend, that was according to the weather forcaster on the television, and so it went, and the evening would be well launched.

Yes, everyone knew Bomber in pubs in the Midlands and the North West when, into one or another of them, Derek would make his entrance most evenings at about nine o'clock and stay no longer than ten thirty, for he had to get up early in the mornings on account of him being a sales rep for Dolliters Wholesale Catering Supplies. Dolliters Wholesale Catering Supplies was famous, as Derek would say, for their cooked meats, smoked ham, honey roasts, Gammon steaks, black puddings, liver sausage, German pepper salami, southern fried chicken fillets, their wide variety of confectionery, ground almonds, raisins, sultanas.

'You name it, we've got it,' he would say.

There was Dolliters' canned fruit, their snacks, crisps, hula hoops, tortilla chips, nuts, crab mayonnaise, their Cornish pasties, coleslaw, hummus, taramasalata, anchovy fillets, black pitted olives, green chilli peppers, canned potatoes, peas, beetroot, the plastic cutlery and the paper plates, the knives, forks, spoons, the floor care products, the washing up liquid, the hand soaps and the whole caboodle. There was everything and anything one might require in terms of catering. Derek could go on listing the products all day. He boasted he knew them all by heart. He let it be known that he was a good rep too, and not only on account of his nineteen stone, although, he maintained, his weight was to his advantage. He fitted the image of the product.

'No good having some skinny bastard doing this job,' he had said on occasion, patting his ample abdomen.

Derek would sit up on one of the high stools at the bar whenever there was room to do so. He liked that best. He would sit on his stool. He would pat his generous stomach, lift it and rest it against the bar counter. That would be it. And Derek would be all set for the evening. He would be well and truly ensconced.

There at the bar he enjoyed the proximity of the real ale pumps, Ansells, M&B, Banks, the draft Fosters and Heineken, the bottles of Bells whisky, Teachers and White and Mackay, the Booths Gin, the Russian Vodka arranged in line in their optics, reflected, light and colours together, in the embossed mirror behind them. He felt at home with the white plastic bowl of ice cubes, the black Ansell ashtrays, the cut lemon in its white saucer, the glossy blue and silver packets of Planters' dry roasted nuts hanging in clusters by the A.G. Motor Repairs calendar.

In the Crown and Mitre outside Burnley, the old Watney's advert with its pure red background, its full pint glass in the foreground, was a throw-back to old times. He liked that. It was a relic. A work of Art. It hung there on the wall adjacent to the bar and against the faded green and red floral wallpaper.

Wherever he went, whatever pub he patronized, Derek would sit or stand up at the bar.

He would call down to his dog, Bomber, 'You want a nice packet of Walkers crisps, Bomber, my love?'

'Two packets of your best Walkers,' he'd request of the landlord or the barman. 'One roasted chicken flavour for yours truly and one beef and onion for the bitch, if you'd be so kind, sir.'

He would pat his opulent beer belly reassuringly.

'Comfortable, that's me. Well-nourished,' he'd bawl.

Well, he meant it as a joke, but also as an excuse for his size, and a means of drawing attention to himself, which is where his old Bomber came in. Bomber broke down barriers. She carved a passage to conviviality.

'Do you mind if I bring the dog in, sir?' he would ask the landlord of a pub he had not as yet visited on his travels, he being off his beaten track.

It might have been a pub in the Border Country or, on occasion, outside Carlisle off the A595. He travelled far and wide, he'd have one know, as a sales rep for Dolliters. He would park in the pub car park or on the forecourt. He would leave the dog in the back of the car, yapping and moaning, and he'd enter the pub, go to the bar, say a nice good evening, which might or might not get a response. He'd order a pint of their Best, and as the barman or landlord poured it, would lean a little forward, and in civil tones enquire: 'Would you mind if I brought the dog in, sir? She's no trouble. She's out there in the car?' If the barman or landlord hesitated, he might add: 'She's no trouble, sir. But no problem if it's against the house rules, sir. Thank you.'

When Bomber was not allowed to enter, Derek would drink up his beer and leave and go off and find some other pub that would allow dogs. He'd not stay on. It was difficult to strike up a conversation of any sort without Bomber. People were reserved by nature, that was Derek's view of the matter.

'That's the British for you,' he'd say.

No, he'd drink up and leave with a 'Thank you very much, guv'nor. No problem. Good night.'

He'd drive on then to another pub, leave the dog in the back of the car, order his drink, ask if the dog could come in, and when the barman or landlord said she could, he'd pay for his pint, leave it standing, go out to the car, put the dog on her lead, and, the dog surging ahead of him, he would return to the bar.

'Come along then, Bomber,' he'd call out as he entered, with a show of keeping his voice down.

'Hold on, you silly dog, hold on,' he'd urge in a jolly sort of way.

And heads would turn. They'd see the dog, see Derek. The dog all in an excitement, a golden retriever, a friendly bouncy dog, a good-natured dog as all could see, and who could resist a dog like Bomber. And hands would touch its head, pat its coat, stroke it under the chin authoritatively as if to say: 'We know dogs,' and Derek would say: 'Come and sit down, you silly animal,' but the dog happily would take no notice, and, well, it would be no stone's throw then for the conversation to start up and go on. It'd be on dogs, dogs the customers knew, or had she, for it was a she, had puppies? And no, Derek would say, she'd been seen to.

'Well, I'm out and about every day, on the road,' he'd say. 'Sales rep for Dolliters Wholesale Catering Supplies, no time to spare for old Bomber to be having offspring.'

And so the conversation might then get onto Sales reps, travelling, the state of the motorways, the weather, the incompetence of public transport which no one ever seemed to use, the car being the thing. Then cars would be the topic of conversation, Jap cars of course, and German cars, and well-reasoned arguments would arise about British cars and how they had or had not improved, and whether or not a Ford Galaxy was in the same class as a Volvo Estate. And before one knew, it was half ten, and Derek and Bomber, who between them had been through half a dozen or more packets of Walkers crisps, and Derek himself through five or six pints of beer, would be off.

'Come on Bomber, come on, you dozy old sod,' Derek would call, struggling to find the lead.

And even those who had not been in his circle that evening would again turn their heads to see the dog, all excitement once again, eager for 'walkies' as she hoped. They'd see the dog jump and wag and shake, and turn around in circles, and all would be saying: 'Good night, all the best.' And Derek, leaving the pub with Bomber to go back to the car, would look forward to his next visit, to enjoy again the company of his new-found friends, for they were all right in there they were. They were pleasant folk. And he'd drive back to his hotel or B&B to get himself and Bomber a bit of the supper he'd stowed away in the bottom of his overnight case, cheese, bread, a cold sausage or two, a nice piece of walnut cake. Or he'd make it to the nearest open fish and chippy and have a large cod and double chips and smuggle them back to his hotel room, and share them with Bomber before retiring to bed, confident that an attack of indigestion, his faithful alarm call, would wake him at five the next morning, so that he could set out nice and early on his calls. Up at five, out of the hotel by six, drive to the next port of call. Breakfast on the way or on arrival in a transport cafe, bacon, eggs, beans, toast, three mugs of tea, sometimes a pudding. He was a hungry man. Bomber was a hungry dog. Bomber and Derek were a pair. They needed each other. The dog, Derek. Derek, the dog. She was his companion, his soul mate. His confidant.

'Shut up, you silly animal,' Derek would shout at her when she fussed to get out of the car on one of their many daily journeys.

'I fancy a bit of grub, Bomber, my old darling,' he'd call to the dog on the back seat. 'What about you? Eh? A nice plate of sausage and chips, and two bloody great gherkins. Very nice. Then we've got to get on, old thing. Can't hang about.'

And the dog understood.

Bomber went and got herself run over. She had been sniffing about outside a B&B near Whitehaven while Derek had been cleaning out the car and she had wandered out into the street and got run over. The driver hadn't stopped. Derek was devastated. He was angry, angry with Bomber, angry with the driver of the car, angry with himself.

That evening he entered a pub he knew well outside Wigton.

'Where's Bomber?' they all wanted to know.

He told them. They were very sympathetic. Their concern gave rise to the problem of owning a dog, to dogs they had known, the danger on the roads, learner drivers, joy-riding, law and order, the death penalty, lawlessness in Great Britain, the strict laws relating to crime and punishment in the Philippines as compared with the softly, softly approach in this country.

Derek entered pubs where he was known and they all wanted to know about Bomber and all were moved by what had happened, and, for a time, conversation was sustained. But Bomber's death could not reasonably continue to be the initiator of social intercourse. Derek continued to go into the pubs he knew but he missed the bustle that his entrance with Bomber had once created, the stir and ebullience. Heads now only briefly turned. Conversation stalled. His evenings became heavy-going. They became duller. He sighed a lot.

He missed Bomber, that was the truth of it. He decided he would replace her. That's what he had to do. It was a matter of urgency. Another dog. Get back to normal, he told himself. He wouldn't buy a puppy. He'd not have the time to house-train or look after a puppy. He'd have to have a grown-up dog, a year old at least.

He saw a card in a newsagent in Harrogate: 'Labrador. Good owner needed. Going abroad.'

It was shiny black. He gave twenty quid for it. The dog, a bitch, was called 'Wendy'. 'Wendy' was no bloody name for a dog, not for Derek's dog.

He spoke to the dog, said to it, there in his hotel room the evening after he had bought it, 'What shall we call you? Eh?'

He decided to call her Bomber Two. He told himself it was good and necessary to have continuity. That's what he told himself. Continuity was the thing. He told Bomber Two about the late Bomber, whom he now referred to as Bomber One, told her at great length about old Bomber, the silly animal, and how she had got run over. Told her that she, Bomber Two, was a sales rep dog now, a travelling animal.

'I hope you like cars, dog,' he said. 'Because we're going to be in a car a bloody lot of the time, my girl.'

She had been lively when he met her, had wagged her tail, lifted herself on her back legs, had pawed Derek's significant abdomen. She had been promising, had Bomber Two.

He took her to the pub that first night, put the lead on her, entered the pub door, had to shove her with his foot, gently enough, to make her go in before him, which she did, but without enthusiasm.

'Come on, you silly animal,' he called out bravely, as if having to control her excitement.

But the animal shuffled in as if reluctant to make herself known, and heads turned, looked down, acknowledged the dog, acknowledged Derek, but without the camaraderie Derek had come to expect with Bomber One.

'The new dog,' he called out.

'Got another dog, have you, Derek?' one of the customers at the bar asked.

'Meet Bomber Two,' Derek announced.

But Bomber Two did not attract attention. No one patted her coat for she didn't after all give them much chance to do so. She lay in one spot, panting a little, and after a moment or two closed her eyes.

'She's tired,' Derek explained.

The following day, he took her to a pub off the A710 to Dumfries and which he had not before visited, but Bomber Two caused no interest in herself or in Derek at all. No matter how much Derek made of her entrance, however much he puffed and blew and called to the animal, no one did more than briefly glance then turn away. Bomber Two was a disappointment. She didn't eat the crisps he threw down for her either, however much he encouraged her to do so. In fact, he was obliged to get down on all fours, his large paunch impeding him, and pick them up and then put them on the bar counter and, apologizing, ask the landlord if he would mind throwing them in the rubbish. The landlord didn't like that. He served Derek his third pint in silence, responding to Derek's expressions of geniality with no more than a grunt. That night, Derek went back to the hotel room earlier than was his custom. The dog wouldn't eat fish and chips. She was finicky about her food. She wanted proper dog food out of a tin.

'A bloody snob you are,' Derek complained.

She was the same wherever Derek took her. She was a write-off.

'I had to give Bomber Two away. She wasn't exactly friendly,' Derek told the landlord of his favourite pub the Crown and Mitre outside Burnley after he had got rid of her. 'I've given her away to the owner of a hotel in Longridge. I told him she was unsuited for travelling. The bloke seemed happy enough to take her off me.'

He sat at the bar clutching his pint of Ansells, picking at a bag of nuts, gaining no familiar comfort and reassurance, no consolation, no sense of well-being from the cut lemon in its white saucer, from the A.G. Motor Repairs calendar, from the bottles of Teachers, Bells, White and Mackay and Booth's Gin in their glistening optics, with their myriad reflections in the embossed mirrors at the back of the bar.

Life was getting him down. Business wasn't so good. Dolliters Catering Supplies weren't selling. And the weather was bloody miserable. Driving at night was becoming more difficult, the lights from oncoming traffic hurt his eyes. The hotels were not what they used to be in the old days. And the pubs were unfriendly. Everyone, Derek claimed, was caught up in himself. They were just thinking of themselves. That was a sign of the times. It was all money these days, all money and greed and self-interest. People had lost the art of camaraderie, of community. And it was a bloody shame. He found himself at home of an evening, or in his hotel if he was on the road, by half-past-eight with the TV on, which he'd never liked, and with half a dozen cans of beer he'd brought in, which he would never have done in the old days. He had never bought in beer to drink at home or in the hotel then. It was out of character. His whole life, he complained to himself, was bloody upside down. And he was short of breath. He was always short of breath on account of his weight, but he was shorter nowadays.

'I can't wait till I retire,' he told the landlord of the Crown and Mitre.

He couldn't wait till he retired, he told himself as he travelled through Wales and up through Cumbria and into North Yorkshire on his own with no one on the back seat to call back to, no one to express himself to but himself. And what was worse, what really upset him, more than he could say or understand or admit to, was that, when he revisited the hotel in Longridge whose owner had taken Bomber Two off him, he saw Bomber Two from his hotel bedroom window, and the dog was romping about in the back garden with the hotel owner's children and one of the hotel staff, and she was full of high spirits, yapping and wagging her tail and causing all sorts of attention to be paid to her. And later in the bar that evening Derek saw her again being made a fuss of by the owner and all number of passing customers. That night, returning to his hotel room, he sighed deeply and wondered what he had done to deserve whatever in the world it was that had befallen him. In the days to come, he felt his heart would give out.

His sales for Dolliters suffered. And head office spoke to him as if from a great distance.

'Life's a bitch,' he muttered to himself.

Derek sat in the Crown and Mitre, his belly up against the bar counter.

'A pint of your very best, landlord, if you please,' he requested.

It was served him in silence.

'Cold weather,' a man wearing a cloth cap, standing at the far end of the bar-counter, said.

He was in his seventies, a large man, out of shape, a man on his own, with a weathered beery look.

The man smiled. Raised a hand in salute.

'Cold weather,' he said.

'Cold for Spring,' Derek agreed.

'You want to buy a dog?' the man enquired.

'No, thanks,' Derek replied. 'But let me buy you a drink,' he added, which generous offer the man accepted thankfully, and then moved in to seat himself on the stool next to Derek.

It was Derek's intention to buy the fellow a pint, stay while he drank it, and then he would go off and get in an early night. That's what he would do, but then, having paid for the man's drink, he asked in a tone of voice that was meant to convey disinterest: 'What sort of dog?'

'Bearded collie,' the man said. 'Lovely creature. Bitch. Belonged to my brother. He and his wife split up. He hasn't the time to look after her. The collie, I mean. Lovely girl, she is. Lovely temperament. A real friend. A beauty. If you're interested.'

'No thanks,' Derek assured the man.

'She'll break your heart,' the man said.

Derek drank from his beer. Put down his glass.

A bearded collie was a fine-looking animal. Collies made loyal companions. Everyone knew that.

'What's her name? he asked.

'Markova,' the man said.

'Markova' s no name for a dog,' Derek said.

AN EVENING MEAL

There she is, waiting for God knows what, and God only knows what she's thinking, Jonathon Barritt said to himself.

They were seated at the dining room table. Dinner had been beef stroganoff followed by Costa Rican Medium Roast coffee. Catherine now with a small cognac, it being Friday. She was wearing her black, low cut dress with three quarter length sleeves. And there was that God-forsaken blank look on her. Looking out as if someone else was sitting opposite her, someone out of Jonathon's view.

He thought, sitting there at the side of the dining table, his one leg crossed over the other, about Catherine's mental state. Not that she hadn't always been more or less unfathomable. He had found, when she was young, her inscrutability rather fetching. Quite sexy, in fact. Made him sort of – well, he'd not go into that. Not now. Now she was fifty. Though, he had to admit, she was well preserved. Did herself out well.

He wondered, seated as he was, smoking a Benson and Hedges, how easy or not it'd be to kill her. Not that he was going to. But she had a long slender neck. It was her neck that had first excited him when they had known each other those many years ago. A sensuous neck, as he now recalled. A neck which could easily be taken between two hands and throttled. It'd be over in a minute. Maybe two, he thought. He wondered whether, while he strangled her – though he knew he wouldn't – whether, while he did, if he did, she would notice.

'Penny for your thoughts,' he said.

'I have none,' she said.

She had, but she was not saying. She had been thinking how much Jonathon had changed, sitting there, neither in nor out of the room. He was weightier, altogether heavier than when they were young. And all that hair he had on his stomach. He hadn't had hair on his stomach when he was young. But now he had. There was his bloated stomach, and there were his chins and varicose veins. And his lack of get-up-and-go.

And she found it more satisfying to concentrate on that evening's 'visitor', who wasn't there, and so couldn't be seen by Jonathon, only by her. He was young. And lean. Without hair on his stomach, seated across the dining table from her. The two of them quietly planning Jonathan's death, how it was best done, and how thereafter to dispose of the body, and how she must, must remember to replant the geranium which only that weekend she had bought from the garden centre.

SARAH

Sarah, coming up to sixty-five. Seated in the armchair under the window in the living room of her flat in West London, waiting for Petra to phone. She could have been a star. People had told her so. And no one could say she hadn't tried, and, looking back, it had been all right. Terrific. Then Gerry died.

It was all right with Gerry. She and Gerry had been a team. He had class. Highly regarded, almost a star. Drank of course, but who didn't in those days. In those days, people drank. Men drank. It was the thing to do. Gerry's Club – not her Gerry – the actors' club – Gerry's – Groucho's – the other one, what was its name? – the other one – closed down now. Joe Allen's, there was always Joe Allen's. Everyone used to go to Joe Allen's, it was the place to go, although sometimes, she went and she'd feel, oh God, this is so fucking awful, all those people, stars, and those hangers on – sometimes she'd feel what was the point? But Gerry and she went. Of course. No point in staying at home in the flat. The flat. It wasn't the sort of place one stayed in for long, not for too long if one could get out, Joe Allen's, the Queen's, the Lamb and Flag. Then Gerry died.

She'd go and see Petra if it wasn't for that God-awful cat of hers, which Petra clearly loved a lot, a lot more than anything or anyone else. That cat with its fur all over one's trousers, all over one's skirt. Moulting, forever moulting, non-stop moulting. She's moulting, Petra said. Christ.

No one seemed to know anyone anymore, Sarah in the armchair under the window thought. No one. No one at all. And the drains. The drains were blocked. The landlord's agent – God knows who the landlord was, someone in far off places, no doubt – the landlord's agent told her she must have put something down there, fat, oil, something that's blocking the drains, as if it was her fault. She didn't use fat or oil, she told them. She phoned them, told them she went out to eat, she didn't cook in the flat. She went out. The drains were stinking the place out. Tuesday night, was it? – she'd been to that show – God, what a bore that was, that show, by the friend of Terry's – it was in verse, for God's sake. She'd got in about twelve and there it was – the drains. Lying in bed with the stinking drains all about her – getting into the bed clothes, into the wardrobe. So now she was in the armchair under the window, waiting for the landlord's agent to send the men about the drains, clean them out, unblock them. So, of course, she wasn't staying in while that was going on. She'd have to go out, even if it was to Petra and her fucking cat and its fur balls, and its hair all over her trousers. She'd go to the Queen's, but that dreadful, dreadful man Philip would be there. He was always there. Might be there. Philip, pompous, self-regarding arsehole, thought he could act, said he was writing his autobiography. Philip, always looking over his shoulder, everyone's shoulder to see if he could spot someone who'd come in who was important. God. Sarah didn't know what had happened, not exactly, couldn't remember, the two of them shouting at each other in The Queen's. It had been him saying about her not paying her way when she could get away with it, always on the cadge – the bastard, saying that. All those people, and him saying she was on the cadge as per usual. And she was shouting at him – shouting he was a total absolute failure – Philip, a nobody. She'd stormed out. She wasn't going back to the Queens, not today. So, it was Petra. She had rung her. On her mobile. Petra. Half an hour earlier. It was her voice mail. She'd tried her again, twice, always Petra's fucking voice mail. So, it was Sarah in her armchair, and the drains, now Gerry was gone.

It was the ciggies that did it for Gerry. Even after he got throat cancer, he smoked, even after he'd had the operation, he'd have a ciggy. He'd always smoked, it's what one did. She had sometimes wondered, it was a nagging thought, whether it was because she didn't smoke, had never smoked, that she hadn't got the work she might have done if she had smoked. One never knew. The slightest thing could put people off. 'She doesn't smoke, you know. She's not the sort we'd want. She's not really right for the part.' No one had actually said that to her, but should they have done so, she thought that she would have said that she was not up for the part of a fucking chimney. She thought, seated in the armchair under the window, that that would have been a jolly good retort.

It had been no good telling Gerry not to smoke. Gerry and ciggies were old friends. Ciggies and Guinness. Thin as a rake, all bones in the last year. People didn't recognize him. 'Oh, my God, Gerald, it's you. How are you getting along?' Bloody silly question. He was fucking dying. Before their eyes, everyone's eyes, dying. All, all bones. Refused to go into hospital at the end. Die at home, he said. Not going into the fucking hospital, he said. They'll fucking kill me in there, he said. They gave him morphine. He died of morphine, a ciggy between his teeth, half a glass of Guinness on the bedside table. Hadn't the strength to finish it.

The phone rang. It was Petra.

She had started to see Dr Reynolds, she told Petra. She couldn't think why she was seeing him. She had gone to the GP with her chest, and he asked how she was getting on since Gerry, and she said sometimes she didn't know why she bothered. The GP said this and that and arranged for her to have Cognitive Behavioural Therapy. She went to a woman at St Ann's, who, God help her, asked so many questions. It was like a fucking exam, she told Petra, when she went over to see her that afternoon, with the fucking cat, its fur all over the place. She went back to the GP surgery – a different GP this time, an Indian – she never saw the same GP twice – one had to take pot luck. The Indian suggested Dr Reynolds. 'A very good man,' he said.

The first time she went to see him, Dr Reynolds had asked her when her husband Gerry had died.

Two years ago, she had said.

'I'm going to this psycho man,' she said to the man who'd come to clean out the drains, an African American from Brixton. He had such a nice smile. Six feet two, she told Petra on the phone. She liked him. His name was Derrick, she said.

Petra wanted her to look after her cat, she said to Derrick who was standing by the drain outside the flat.

Petra was going to stay with her son in Worcester. His wife had walked out on him and he was in a state, and would Sarah look after her cat Carlos, her fucking cat, for two weeks? Her fucking cat Carlos, its fur everywhere, all over the flat, God knows where.

She said to Dr Reynolds, how could she refuse?

So now Carlos was living with her. And she had to feed him disgusting pork and salmon in jelly. And Petra had said to her, don't forget the water. And let him out to do his business, but don't let him out at night. The bloody cat under her feet.

The flat was not big enough for them both, she told Dr Reynolds, him sitting there, the consulting room blinds half down, his trousered legs stretching out into the room, his face in shadow, so she didn't really know what he was thinking, and at some point, she wasn't quite sure he hadn't fallen asleep.

She told Derrick, when he had come back the following morning to clean out the drains, that Dr Reynolds hardly ever spoke. All she got from him was the odd word, the occasional murmur, and so she was left to do the talking, she said to him.

She was in the kitchen and she had called the cat 'Gerry'. Just like that. Out it came. 'Gerry'. What was she thinking? she said to herself. She thought of telling Dr Reynolds the next time she saw him. She could have told Derrick when he came back again to try to fix the drains, but he had a workmate with him, a skinny little white man whom she didn't take to. The fucking cat had got on the kitchen surfaces by the sink and had knocked a cup onto the floor and she had yelled 'for fuck's sake, will you stop farting about, Gerry. Christ's sake, if you can't stop your moping around, not knowing what to do with yourself, then fuck off to the pub. Moaning, complaining no work, for Christ's sake.' – and, without thinking, she'd let it out at the back, and Petra had said, she was sure she had said, don't let it out after dark. And she had. She was out there in the back garden looking for it, but it had fucked off. Fuck off then, she had shouted into the night.

Would it be all right if she called him James? she said to Dr Reynolds. Such a nice name. She was waiting to hear from her agent, James, darling, she said. She'd been to a casting. For a commercial. She'd been in at nine thirty and had still been there at eleven. A cattle market, James, she said. Ghastly. That's how it was now, that was what it had come to. Thousands of them waiting, she said. Dozens of them. Women of a certain age. A young man, who didn't look more than twelve years old, asked her what she had been doing, she told Dr Reynolds, and Dr Reynolds said 'Ah'.

Dr Reynolds said 'Ah', she told Petra when she phoned to find out how the cat was settling in. Oh, it was fine, Sarah said. She didn't tell her it had fucked off.

Her bedroom ceiling had fallen in, she told Petra who phoned from her son's house in Worcester. She wasn't surprised, she said. She had complained more than once to the landlord's agent about the cracks. She had been in the kitchen and the ceiling in the bedroom had come crashing down. All over her bed, she said to Petra. So, now she had the builders in. Mike and a man called Beck or Bock or someone. A name she couldn't get her head around.

Before Gerry, she said to Dr Reynolds, there had been others of course. When one was young, and on tour, that was what happened, she said.

Before Gerry, there was Simon, baritone, big voice. Solid, reliable, chorus at Covent Garden, Glyndebourne, she said to Derrick who was down inside the drain, knocking out the bricks.

Before Gerry, there had been Simon, a very good baritone, but awfully dull in himself, she told Mike and Mike's mate Beck or Bock or whatever his name was, as they were pulling down the remaining plaster, and saying something unintelligible about 'drywall' and a 'botched job'.

Before Simon there was Terence. None of them were Gerry. None. He had a tongue on him, had Gerry, she said to Dr Reynolds, who sat there and hardly said a word, so it was up to her. But she felt better after she'd been to see him, walking out of his consulting room, walking to the Tube station. Although, when she thought about it, she wasn't sure she'd recognize him if she ever met him in the street.

She told Derrick outside the flat by the drains that Dr Reynolds reminded her of Gerry.

She told Dr Reynolds himself that he reminded her of Gerry. She didn't know why she had said that. He didn't remind her of Gerry. But she said it.

She was wearing Vinaigre de Toilette that afternoon which was from a nineteenth century recipe and contained an infusion of plants, woods and spices, she said to Derrick as he drank the cup of tea she had made for him. A perfume that was rather too pungent for her liking, she said.

She told Mike and his mate Beck or Bock, the Vinaigre de Toilette had been sold to her by a sales woman in Selfridges.

She guessed the sales woman's face had not been fully in evidence since the sales woman had first discovered the obliterating benefits of applying excessively generous amounts of foundation cream and blush and so forth.

She had formulated and practised this observation on her own in the kitchen over a six o'clock gin and tonic. Mostly gin, less tonic. Once perfected, she conveyed her descriptive account first to Mike, then, more importantly to her, to Derrick, and subsequently to Dr Reynolds, and was thinking of trying it out on Petra on the phone but, by the time Petra phoned again to ask about the fucking cat who, unknown to her, had of course fucked off, Sarah had become bored with the whole thing and was no longer certain it sounded all that clever. So, she didn't.

She had seen a woman in a blue wool coat, she told Dr Reynolds. She had thought the coat too large for her. But anyway, there she was on the platform's edge at Baker Street. As her train had come in, the woman had thrown herself onto the tracks, which was why, James, darling, Sarah said, she was a little late that afternoon.

The drains were all right now, Derrick said to Sarah. Brickwork and piping had come away, and there had been a sewage build up. But it was all done now, he said, and it was nice to have met her and thanks for the teas and all the best, and Sarah thanked him and felt she would miss him, although she didn't say so. The next day it was Mike who said his mate Beck had finished the painting of the new ceiling. It was a nice job, he hoped she'd agree, and she had agreed, and thanks for the teas and nice to have met her, and take care, Mike said, and his mate Beck, whom she now quite liked, said take care, and she waved them off in their van, as she was standing on the pavement outside the front of the house, waving. Waving. And quietly calling goodbye.

Dr Reynolds had left, she was told by reception. Why was that? she asked. No reply. Her enquiry ignored. She was to join Dr Leone Hoffman's group. She was directed to where the group was assembled. She looked in. Dr Hoffman was sitting at the front behind a desk, patients seated in rows before her. An angry young man ranting. She turned away and left the building.

She was seated in the armchair under the window. She heard someone at the back door. She opened it. It was Petra's cat. He had decided to come back home, had he? Sarah said to it. Fucking about out there. God help her, he was impossible.

Petra phoned. How was the cat? she asked. Oh, Sarah said. Gerry was fine.

CITY WALK

There were twelve of them. They were walking about the City close to St Paul's looking out for trees. The Sweet Gum Tree, the London Plane, the Judas Tree, New Horizon Elms, Ginkos from China. Some of the trees weren't to be discovered.

'That's it, the Foxglove Tree,' the leader of the group said. 'No, no, it isn't. It should be there. My map tells me it should be.'

The sun shining on a warm Sunday morning. Down side streets, away from tourists milling around St Paul's. Twelve of them all over seventy, some in their eighties.

One of their number, David Partiker, had volunteered to be 'the back stop' so as to make sure no one got left behind.

Hidden squares of the City. Quite small. Many a surprise. The Postman's Square with the plaques commemorating those who lost their lives in trying to save others. A boy drowned trying to save his little brother. So many drownings. And fires. A mother died rushing back into her blazing house to save her children. Plaque after plaque. Quiet heroes. Mid 1800's – 1977.

'We'll have a cup of tea in the café now, shall we?' the leader of the group said.

Coffees, teas, biscuits, from a stall nearby.

On they went. The tiered garden tucked away by the Worshipful Guild of Barbers. The sky blue. The elderly band, ten women, two men. Always the same – women but few men. Men dead or at home and unwilling to go out, or too poorly. The London Wall, Friday Street, Number 1 Love Lane, Meryll Lynch, Aldermanbury, names which carry history forward. Little Britain, Aldersgate Street, St Martin's Le Grand.

'Have you seen David Partiker? Where's David?'

David in his beige raincoat and rain hat. Stooping David. He was supposed to be 'back-stop', bringing up the rear, to make sure no one went astray. His wife died last year. It had hit him hard, that was the general opinion. He wasn't one for talking about it. Pleasant enough though. It was said he slept with his late wife's nightie in the bed beside him.

Where was David?

Two of the women went back to have a look for him. The others waited, standing about on the pavement in Wood Street.

'Where have those two gone?' someone asked.

They'd gone to find David.

A woman with red hair, not her own colour – used to be when she was younger, but no longer – went off to find the two women who had gone to find David.

'Where's she going?' some of them asked.

'To find the other two who are looking for David.'

'Christ,' someone muttered.

The general atmosphere between them was not improving.

'I've an appointment with my dentist this afternoon,' said a woman wearing a head scarf and carrying in each hand a plastic carrier bag.

Eight of the twelve walkers standing about, looking left and right, marooned in Wood Street.

David turned up. He came into sight from around a corner unexpectedly. It was David. Such a relief.

'Where've you been? We were worried.'

'Have you seen the others?'

David in his beige raincoat stood there helpless.

'I went to have a look at the display in the glassware shop in the street down there,' he said.

The question arose, should they now wait for the other two and for the woman with red hair. Should they wait?

'My wife,' said David, 'loved glassware.'

They were standing about, blocking the pavement. Young women in short shorts with their legs on display, passing by, stepped around them and into the road.

An unspoken question arose: would they too do this walk one day? When they're elderly? It couldn't be imagined. They were so young. Old age for them so distant in time. But they would. Some would. With their legs covered up, a woolly cardigan drawn to, buttoned up the front. Good walking shoes. The occasional pain in the hip. And was today's elderly walking group ever young? Oh, yes, and they too wore short shorts. In the sixties. Not in the fifties. In the fifties, mostly, as some of them would seem to remember, it would have been skirts and the men would have been wearing ties.

The nine of the twelve including David in the walking group waited.

And there was the red headed woman and the other two now. They were all there. What a relief.

'Don't go wandering off again like that, David.'

It was said he visited his wife's grave every day.

'I'm trying to find the Silver Lime. It's on my map. But it doesn't seem to be here,' the group leader said. 'Are you with us, David?'

Physically, David was with the walking group and at the same time in his head he was with his late wife. He wouldn't say, but he had seen her in the shop that sold glassware. He had turned to look at the display in the window and there she had been, looking sad and bedraggled, and at a loss. Then, after a moment or two, he had seen that it had been himself. He had been seeing the reflection of himself in the shop window. He had tried to see her again, but he couldn't.

The woman with red hair had taken the opportunity, while being absent from the group, while looking for David, to telephone her husband at home. How was he? Not too good, he had said. She knew her husband was unwell, but from time to time she needed to get away from him.

'I'll not be very long. Just phone me on my mobile if you need to,' she had said.

There they were, all together again. At last. All reassembled, safely reunited.

'There's a café along by the station,' the leader of the group said to everyone. 'If you're off home, there's the station or some of you might like to have a coffee and a sandwich or something.'

The woman with red hair sighed. She would have a quick cup of coffee and a sandwich and then go off to the Portrait Gallery, then home to her husband. She, along with a few others, followed the leader to the café.

Most of the walkers went home.

David returned to the window of the shop selling glassware.

SPRING AWAKENING

In the town of Bouvolieu, South West of Clermont-Ferrand, in the week following the 3rd anniversary celebrations commemorating the end of the Second World War, from the tops of poles and from buildings the flags are flying.

Christiane Aubert, in her mother's apartment above Madame Bonnaire's small convenience store on the corner of the Rue de Verrier, plays the upright piano. Her mother knits. She is seated on the hardback upholstered seat against the wall. The armchair of a darkly floral design in the corner of the room remains empty. It once belonged to the mother's late husband who died during the Italian Campaign in Sicily. He is an ever-present absence; everywhere and nowhere. The piece the daughter plays is a Chopin Etude. The garments the widow is knitting are bed socks against the cold nights, against the loss of warmth of her late husband, her feet tucked into his, his hand on her hip, his body moving over heavily on hers those Sunday afternoons when he was not out drinking with the men. The Etude comes to an end. 'Play it again,' the mother says to her grown-up daughter.

Danielle Fournier is in the park with everyone else. And being with everyone else she feels she is part of humanity, part of nature, of the gradual reawakening after the years of destruction, fear and isolation. The need and desire to get out and about, to start over again. The May cherry trees and magnolia are still in full blossom. Men and women, children and dogs, the whole world is out on a Sunday, rejoicing at the freedom after the long hard years of war. New clothes have been bought; old favourites brought out. New confidence shines in the way the people walk, the time they take for themselves. People are singing. A band is playing.

Then she sees him. Albert Legrand. Her betrothed. Joined the First Free French Division in 1940, fought in Tripoli. Wounded. His beautiful cornflower blue eyes blinded, she had been told. There he is, slender of build as she remembers him. Now a little bent at the shoulders. And there is his dog. In this moment she feels the war that took him away lasted not the four years but a lifetime. And there is a woman at his side.

She had made her enquiries. He had been hospitalized in Algiers. Later she learnt he had married his nurse. She had wished him dead then. He had gone against his promise to her. In surviving, he had killed her, she has said.

And there he is, with the dog and with the woman on his arm.

Danielle Fournier begins to shake. She sits awhile to steady herself. She leaves the gardens and returns home.

In the garden of the large house on the corner of the Place de la Mairie, Monsieur and Madame Pelletier are sharing a moment in their recently re-furbished conservatory, greenery and Spring flowers everywhere. Monsieur Pelletier is leaning on the back of the dark wooden seat on which his wife Silviane is seated.

'Do you want to go to the park for a walk?' he says. 'Go and listen to the band?'

'No,' she says.

He has anticipated her reply.

She has not spoken more than a few words for weeks.

He had not had an affair, he had insisted. He had had to go to Lille for a business meeting, had had to stay overnight at the Hôtel Renard as he had missed his train. The fact that a female colleague was also staying at the hotel was no more than a coincidence. It was the truth, so God help him, he had said.

It is not as if Silviane hadn't believed him. She had. It's not as if she has any doubt concerning her husband's fidelity. She hasn't. If only she did. If only he had had an affair, she has thought, then she wouldn't feel so bored, so without interest, without distraction from the uneventful life she has had to endure, living as they are in this small commonplace town so as to be near her husband's ailing mother.

It is unbearable. Everyone else is in Paris, busily occupied, having fun, their lives full of scheming and manoeuvring. How she misses all this. When they were living in Paris, in Belleville, every day seemed full of intrigue; her sister Marie's divorce, the murder of her friend Angélique's drug addicted cousin, the fire at the Brausin's house in Passy, who was and who wasn't invited to Leonard's or Dorian's.

The question has arisen: how can she enliven her own dull existence? She can hardly compel her husband, who is leaning on the back of the conservatory seat, to have an affair. The thought has occurred to her that she might herself take a lover, but she could never find it in herself to be disloyal. That is what she has told herself. Apart from which, since they've moved to their present disheartening locality, there hasn't been a man with whom she could possibly have entertained having an affair, and, truth to tell, there hasn't been any man who has expressed any interest in having an affair with her. It isn't as if she's physically plain. She knows that. A pretty enough face. It is, perhaps, she has thought, her lack of conversation. She can't always find things to say. And anyway, most people she knows, she has told herself, are nowadays so self-obsessed and show no real interest in anyone but themselves.

'A telegram, Monsieur,' the maid calls out as she enters the conservatory.

He opens the telegram.

'I'm to return to Paris. Company business. I have to be there for some months,' he says. 'Shall you come, Silviane? We can take mother. With the warmer days now, she is feeling a lot better. Shall you come?'

'Yes,' she says.

She rises from the conservatory seat.

'And now,' he says, 'Shall we walk in the park and listen to the band?'

'Yes,' she says, as she takes his arm.

Everything is changed. The past forgotten.

Madame Tremblay is watching her friend's little boy Jacques riding on the Merry-Go-Round at the funfair near the Rue de la Fontaine. She loves the child; such a lively imaginative little fellow. He often spends the day with her. She watches as the boy waves to her.

As she waves back to him, she remembers the young man Philippe.

'We must run away together,' she recalls him saying to her.

They had been seated at the table on the 'terrasse' of his father's restaurant Les Toits Rouges.

'We must run away together,' he said. So eager. So intent. Such a young man, and she nearly twice, well, almost twice, perhaps not nearly twice his age, she thinks.

She lunches at Les Toits Rouges once, sometimes twice a week, her husband being in Marseilles on business. She likes the food, simple, tastefully presented and a small glass of Picpoul-de-Pinet.

She has her friends, women of her own age, in their forties, some of them with children. Her own child, Tomas, is with her first husband in Montpellier. Tomas said he preferred it there but, of course, it was, she believes, what his father had told him to say.

'But I'm married,' she had said to Philippe.

He'd walked over and sat at her table. His blonde hair falling forward, his eyes seeking hers.

She has to admit to herself she had enjoyed his protestations of love, his youthful desire. Of course, naturally. But it is ridiculous to think the two of them could run away, goodness gracious, or even have an affair. There are her friends and the boy's father; impossible. And, anyway, it wouldn't work. He'd tire of her. He is nineteen. Ludicrous.

He had his arm on the back of her chair.

Without looking behind her, she had known his father was looking in their direction.

'Philippe,' she had said. 'You are very nice, and very handsome, and endearing. But I am married.'

'Your husband has another woman,' Philippe said to her.

In all likelihood he had, she had thought. The probability had occurred to her, his business trips, his protestations of tiredness. They had been married five years. Men had their relationships. That was what they did. It had happened to her friends, to Monique, and Monique and her husband had only been married two years. And Natalie, married to the Brazilian, had herself had lovers. But Natalie was the type who would take lovers even had she been married to the most wonderful and the richest man in the world.

'I love you,' Philippe said. 'Please get that into your head. I love you. And I am not going to give up on you.'

'Oh, dear.'

His father in his white apron was at their table.

'Good afternoon. A lovely sunny day.'

'It is,' she said.

'I hope my boy Philippe is not troubling you.'

'No. Only I have to go. Errands to see to. Shopping to do. My husband returns from Marseilles this evening.'

Philippe removed his arm from the back of her chair.

'You have made everything out here so pleasant,' she said to the boy's father. 'The shrubbery. The flowers. The blue and purple Hyacinth, the pink and mauve Irises.'

'It's Spring,' he said.

'It is indeed,'

'Philippe, your mother requires your help with the linen,' he said.

Philippe shrugged, rose, and left without a word.

His father, straightening his apron, took his place at the table.

'May I offer you a liqueur?' he asked her.

'No, no, that is very kind, but I must have no more.'

'You have such beautiful eyes,' he said to her, his arm across the back of her chair.

She remembers thinking, 'It's Spring. It's May. The 3rd anniversary of the end of the war. Love is in the air.'

She sees now Jacques' funfair ride has finished. He is running over towards her, fearlessly. His life before him. He wants to go on the Merry-Go-Round again. On a day such as this, no simple pleasure can be denied.

Danielle Fournier waits outside the open door of her house in the Rue du Marechal. And there they are, her friend Madame Tremblay and Jacques.

The boy sees his mother and runs to her.

'I've been on the Merry-Go-Round, twice, Maman,' he calls.

His cornflower blue eyes sparkling as he speaks.

Danielle Fournier sweeps him up in her arms and holds him close to her chest.

Christiane in the narrow hallway of her mother's apartment above Madame Bonnaire's small convenience store on the corner of the Rue de Verrier pulls on her outdoor shoes in readiness. The boy Philippe is at the door. They walk to the river. They stop by the boat house. Philippe puts a hand on her breast. She gasps, pushes it away.

'But I love you,' he says.

Christiane knows he probably says that to everyone.

Hesitantly, she takes his hand and places it on her left breast above her heart.

From further along the embankment people can be heard calling out to each other and singing Le Chant Des Partisans.

FROM ACROSS THE SEA

She is waiting for her son in the hallway of her flat in the seaside town where she lives. She is ninety-three years old. She's wearing a stylish green-check wool and cashmere overcoat, a matching scarf and her four-inch heels.

'You're late, are you? It's lovely to see you. It's been so long,' she says.

'Two weeks,' he says.

'You look tired.'

'I'm fine.'

He waits as she checks her appearance in the mirror by the front door. She's preparing herself for her entry to the world beyond. She smiles and flutters her eyelids at her reflection.

Quite early in adulthood, she decided to take ten years off her life, the ten years being the number she spent in the hated Children's Home, so that, when she was fifty, she had it understood she was forty. When she reached her mid-eighties, she gave up the conceit, deciding her great age lent her gravitas and the right to additional respect and privilege.

'Is that a new coat?' he asks. 'You look very elegant as usual.'

'Thank you for the compliment, dear,' she says. 'The coat is quite old. You possibly don't recognize it as, on account of you so rarely coming to see me, it's not often I have the opportunity to wear it.'

He holds her arm as they descend the stairs to the ground floor and slowly walk to the front of the block.

'What a nice car,' she quietly exclaims as if she has never seen it before.

He helps her into the front passenger seat, fastens her seat belt.

'And so comfortable,' she remarks.

'I'm glad to see you're wearing a tie,' she says to him as he turns the key in the ignition.

'I'm not going back to that nursing home,' she says, as they drive through the town to the sea front. 'They tied me to the dining room chair.'

'They said you were rocking backwards and forwards,' he says.

She has been in and out of the nursing home on several occasions this year. When she's unable to look after herself, she telephones, takes a taxi and books herself in.

'I'm not going back, make no mistake. That awful food they serve. And all those old people,' she says.

They are in his car, looking out at the cold grey North Sea.

She is remembering her father, him saying to her mother he had met someone else. They were in Pennsylvania. They were travelling across Canada and The States where he was promoting his innovative fruit canning machinery. He didn't see her standing in the kitchen doorway, until he turned, and there she was. She was five years old.

He'd met someone else, he said, and they sailed back to Liverpool on the SS Tunisian, third class, without him; their mother, her sister Frances, her brothers Walter and Robert. She went up on a deck where she wasn't supposed to go. 'Don't you go up there where you don't belong, Helen,' she was told. Frances and Walter wouldn't go up. Robert was just a baby, two years old, born in Ontario on the 3rd of September 1910. But she went. Gritted her teeth, said she was going. Everyone up there in smart suits and dresses. She went up there again, and was shooed away. She was a fighter, that was what was said of her.

They were in the Children's Homes for ten years. Walter and Frances in the Home in Kings Norton. She and Robert in the Home outside Aston. Accommodation for pauper children. 'Don't cry, girl,' the hated matron scolded. 'Your baby brother isn't crying.' The dormitories; dark wood, metal bedsteads. Girls trained to go into service, boys trained in shoemaking, carpentry. Soup on Thursdays, always Thursdays. Fish, Fridays; 'What sort of fish?' 'It's fish, child.' Boiled beef twice a week; 'Chew it well, child, it'll strengthen your teeth'. Mauve print frocks, white pinafores. Pink frocks on Sundays. Their own clothes taken away. Everyone dressed the same.

Parents and relatives permitted four visits a year, on the first Wednesday of every third month. Every visitors' day, they'd assemble in the main hall. There was such excitement. 'He's coming,' Robert would say. In such a state, on one leg and then the other. 'When's visitors' day, Helen?' he'd say to her. He was housed in the building across the drive. They'd meet after school, in the school yard at the back, find a place by themselves. 'Daddy's coming, Helen,' he'd say. He didn't come, not the once in ten years. Robert never accepted he was dead. He would cry and cry, and she'd say, 'He'll be here next time,' because she couldn't say to him, 'He's died', as her mother had everyone believe. 'You'll make it worse for yourselves, for us, if you say about him and that woman,' mother said. And who wanted worse?

Mother worked in the kitchens of the Children's Homes. 'So as to be near you,' she said. Four days of the week at Kings Norton, three days at Robert's and her Home in Aston. It was only going to be for a while, until she got things properly sorted out, she said. Then she said they couldn't afford the rents. And if they did find the money to rent, they'd have to share with other families, the toilets, and the water. No proper kitchen. Cook on a fireplace. They'd all be in one room. Two at most. They'd be better off where they were, she said.

'I can see Daddy now,' Robert used to say. They'd be sitting in the gardens at the back, sitting in the room along from the main hall. He'd say, 'I can see him. He's coming to visit us.' 'We're going back to Pennsylvania,' he said. 'We'll go one day. After the war. The war will be over soon.' she said to him. 'I'm going over there to find him,' he said. He was seven years old. He was going over there to find him when he was big, he said. He died of a heart attack at the age of twenty-one outside the shop in Acocks Green.

'You won't remember your father,' mother said.

She looks out at sea and remembers him; Christmas in Pennsylvania, him with his sack of goodies, a great jumble of presents littering the floor, his great shining red face, the huge grin – was it that large? – was it only large to her? His raucous rendering of 'Happy Christmas to you.' 'Happy Christmas to the little lady,' meaning her. Happy Christmas. And she crying with the happiness at being singled out. He lifts that giant sack above his head, opens it up, all in one go, the presents cascading, tumbling out over the floor.

'The trouble with men is that they have to keep on getting rid of their sperm,' she says now to her son, as they look across the sea towards the horizon.

A ship, unidentifiable, can be seen in the far distance.

'It looks as if it's going out. Norway,' he says.

'I've been listening to that late-night phone-in chat show,' she says. 'They discuss so many things you'd never believe existed. They have discussions on lesbianism and homosexuality, on a thing called S and M which sounds rather troubling and which I do hope you don't contemplate in any way. There are so many people out there who plainly are very lonely, desperate and full of anger. I think quite a lot of them are insane,' she says.

The ship is more clearly visible now. A passenger ship, she thinks.

'I've bought my cleaner a car,' she says.

'What?'

'I believe it's a Ford. Ten thousand pounds.'

'Why have you bought your cleaner a car?' he asks.

'She comes by bus,' she says. 'She tells me the bus company has reduced the frequency of the service and she doesn't think she can come to me anymore. So of course, I've had to buy her a car. She and her husband have gone on a driving holiday to the South of France.'

'You can't afford to buy people cars,' he says.

'Of course, I can. Your father's life insurance, his pension and his investments,' she says stiffly.

Her jaw is set against argument.

After a while she says, 'I had to call the police last night. I couldn't turn over in bed. I phoned them, told them to come along and turn me over.'

'Did they?' he asks.

'They've been three times altogether. Very useful.'

'They won't want to keep coming out,' he says.

'They said they couldn't keep coming, that I should get someone to stay overnight, a carer or some such person. I don't like carers. I had a carer.'

'I know you have,' he says.

'No. I had. I don't have a carer anymore,' she says. 'I got her through a private agency. She was supposed to come in the mornings and in the evenings. But she was always late – sometimes a day late; and never stayed the full hour and she was never the same person. She changed daily: black, white, Asian, European, Romanian, Aborigine. Philippino. The Philippino was nice. Only she stole my earrings.'

'Are you sure?'

'Well, they're not where I put them,' she says. 'So, I wouldn't have her again. I said to the woman at the agency the ones they've sent me won't do. She said they haven't got any more. I've had them all.'

'How many carers do they have on their books?' he says.

'Oh, thousands,' she says.

She has a smile for him specially now, mischievous and conspiratorial.

She watches the ship disappear over the horizon.

She was twenty-three, a nurse at the Manchester Royal Infirmary, and her father turned up, out of the blue, outside the hospital.

Her mother had told everyone he was dead. That was what Helen, Frances and the boys were to say, her mother said. Women who were abandoned by their husbands, brought shame upon themselves. 'Social outcasts' were the words she used.

He was standing in the road, overweight, wearing a scruffy grey suit and brown shoes. He was back from America, he said. It'd been all right out there. Only it hadn't worked out and he'd been back in Britain for three years.

'I've been here in Manchester, seeing about a job,' he said.

He'd been passing by the hospital and had thought he had heard someone call her name.

'You're dead,' she said.

She turned away and left him at the roadside.

'You're cold,' her son says. 'Shall we go to the Garden Centre for a cup of coffee?'

'Oh, yes – you are a good boy,' she says, as if the idea is an unexpectedly new one, although going to the Garden Centre is what they always do when he visits.

'Not many customers,' she says as he drives into the Garden Centre car park. 'It's the time of year, I expect.'

They make their way to the café. They find a table and sit opposite each other.

'I've bought a mobile telephone,' she says, showing him. 'I know how to use it. So useful when you're out and about.'

He steadies her hand as she lifts her cup of coffee and draws it to her mouth and sips.

'Is it too hot?'

'No. I can manage, thank you,' she says.

In the Garden Centre shop, she chooses the chocolate bars.

'Not those, they have nuts in them,' she says.

She chooses two jars of marmalade.

'Not the thick cut, it gets stuck in my teeth. I shall have a packet of that cereal stuff. What's it called? Mussolini.'

'Muesli.'

'I'll have a packet of that – the Mussolini,' she says.

She chooses some biscuits. It takes a long time.

She could have married the doctor at the hospital. She can't remember his name. He said he was going to be a Christian Missionary in China. 'Marry me and we'll go together,' he said. He was nice. A clear open face. But she didn't want to be a Christian missionary or go to China. Instead, she married a civil servant, a professional gentleman, and she threw her nursing certificates to the back of the fire.

She is sitting in her chair by the French windows in the small living room of her first floor flat. Her son is seated opposite her. Everything is in place. There are flowers on a side table.

'We'll have a drink before you go,' she says.

He pours her a large sweet martini and for himself a scotch.

'The television is on the blink,' she says. 'It goes on and off. I give it a kick and it comes on again. That's what you have to do, you know. A sharp kick, that's the way. I have five radios, one for each room. It saves getting up and moving them. I sometimes have them all on at the same time. Although not always on the same programme. One likes a little variety. Here's to us,' she says, raising her glass.

'Here's to us,' he says.

'I've met a very nice lady, an American,' she says. 'She has an apartment on the other side of the block. She brought me a plant. I've put it out on the balcony. A geranium. Pink. Most kind of her. She asked after you. I told her you came up to see me from time to time. She said she was very impressed. Oh yes, I said, my son will do anything for anyone, so long as it fits in with his plans. I would have liked you to have met her, but she's had to go to London to see her dentist.'

She has another Martini, he another scotch.

'You are a dear,' she says. 'I have enjoyed today. You should really get more sleep. You look tired. Do come again soon.'

After he's gone, she takes a taxi to the sea front. She looks out at uninviting sea. The night's drawing in. No ships out there now.

After a while, she telephones and has another taxi take her to the Nursing Home.

CARMIL FORRESTER

She had had rhinoplasty, liposuction, tummy tuck, botox, breast augmentation, face lift, eyelid surgery and laser resurfacing. She had been tattooed. She had a Si Jap Sleeve over her right shoulder and upper arm, golden butterflies on her right hip, hibiscus across her lower back, a scorpion on her left leg below the knee, and honeysuckle in red, orange and blue on one side of her belly.

She came out of Amanda Darling's beauty salon, having endured the full Brazilian, her hair, her face, her nails all done, and she was not what she had been before she'd gone in. That's how it was with Carmil Forrester. It was her contention that a Brazilian, Hollywood style, was more pleasing, more gratifying than sex. The removal by Sharon of her pubic hair by means of waxing and stripping was the most breathtakingly erotic feeling she had ever experienced. She had had it done twice before and, of course, she had had to wait till the hair grew back, and it seemed to take ages to do so, ages and ages, before she could again embark on the experience.

Leaving the salon, as she walked along the High Street, Carmil's identity lay in her defoliated pubic bone area. It was there, in the few hours ahead, that she felt alive to a sense of the woman she was.

She was not the girl she had been, not the daughter of Fred and Jenny Forrester of Little Road, Chingford.

It was there in the High Street, as she was about to hail a taxi, that she caught sight of William. She wasn't sure he recognized her.

'It's me,' she called.

'It's me,' she repeated, as William, a tall chap in his early forties whom she had slept with at one time or another and who was married but what of that, moved in towards her and opened his arms in greeting.

'Hey,' he said. 'You look good!'

'Thank you,' she replied, gratified but not altogether believing.

'You look good,' he repeated.

'It's Carmil,' she said.

'Sure. Sure. Of course. Carmil,' he said.

'Where've you been?' he asked.

'Beauty salon,' she said.

'You can tell,' he said with a grin, which unsettled her.

At that moment, before William could say anything further or suggest they went for a drink or whatever, a woman of about thirty, that is of Carmil's age, and who was approaching her, stopped and said, 'Hey! Hey! How are you doing?! You're on Facebook. We're Facebook friends! Isn't that terrific?!'

'Oh, yes, sure is!' Carmil said. 'Fancy us bumping into each other like this!'

'Yeah! We've got to post about this. Like, I'm going to post about this when I get home!'

'Right. Me too!' said Carmil.

'Got to rush,' the woman said. 'Late – appointment – Amanda's beauty salon.'

And with that she went on her way.

'Hey. A Facebook friend,' William said.

'Yes,' said Carmil.

'What's her name?'

'I don't know. I've never met her in my life. I've thousands of them. It's awesome'

'You want a drink or something. Something would be nice,' he said.

Not 'something', she thought, not with my Brazilian.

'A drink. Then I have to go,' she said.

William was cool, he was neat. But it hadn't lasted more than six weeks.

It was the same with all of her boyfriends. She took them on and kept them tight until they lost their shine. Then she dropped them wherever they were, whenever it occurred to her to do so. They might be walking along the street, coming out of a club, the movies, been shopping.

She'd say, 'I've had enough.'

'Enough?'

'Of you. It's over.'

'Over?'

'Us. Finis.'

'Why?'

'Oh, God. If you don't know why, it's no good me telling you.'

That was her way. Her way with men. She didn't explain further. She declined to elaborate, because she was unable to do so. All she knew was the fellow had 'lost his shine', was of no interest to her any longer, was dispensable, a nuisance, needed to be unloaded, there and then in the road, on the pavement, wherever.

'Goodbye,' she said to them.

And that was that.

They would be left with their mouths open, a frown on their faces, and standing there in anger.

She had made enemies. The day would come, some of her friends, her girlfriends, said, when someone would bring her to her knees.

Her ambition was to be on a TV Reality Show. To be a celebrity. If she was a celebrity, she told herself, she'd know who she was.

Carmil met Ed. Ed was as sharp as a razor, vicious, lean and angular. Boastful. A thug. He wore a koi sleeve tattoo on his right arm, a geisha back piece, a dragon neck tattoo. On their second date, back at his place, he pushed her into the bathroom, grabbed her by the hair, held her face into the sink, washed and wiped all the Amanda Darling from her face until she glowed pink and sore and then he dragged her to his bed. She'd not felt so secure in all her life. She began to dream of marriage.

Then he said to her – they were outside The Blue Club in Stockton at four in the morning – he said: 'It's over.'

'What?'

'Over. Finis. Ta-ta.'

He hailed a taxi, and left her standing on the pavement with her mouth open.

The next day she went back to Amanda Darling's beauty salon.

'Is Sharon free?' she asked.

'Hi there, Shar,' Amanda Darling called to Sharon. 'Carmil's here for a Brazilian.'

'Hi, Carmil,' Sharon called over.

Carmil had Ed's baby. A boy. She wasn't going to tell Ed. But she'd thought how nice it would be having a baby, that it would make her feel better than she had been, more the person she hoped herself to be. It was born with tattoos on its face and neck. The doctors said something about 'port-wine stain' or something about a blood or heart disorder. She couldn't remember which or quite what it was they said. But whatever it was, she couldn't handle it. Carmil gave it to her mother and father in Chingford. They looked after it. Took it back and forth to the hospitals, nurtured it like it was their own. It spiced up their old age.

Carmil's father said to the neighbours, 'The baby's doing famously. A lovely kid.'

'Gorgeous,' Carmil's mother said. 'When he's older we're going to have him tattooed with a small yellow butterfly on the left shoulder. Very distinctive,' she said.

'And we've given the kid a piercing, an ear tag,' Carmil's father said.

'A pretty little silver stud. In his left ear,' said Carmil's mother.

'That's what they do these days,' Carmil's father said. 'We've got to keep up with the times.'

HOLDING ON

He was rather grand in his illness, seated in his wheelchair, looking dapper in jacket, tie, light trousers, maroon socks, classic Oxford brogues. An elderly gentleman waiting for a CT scan. His outward display intended, if not altogether consciously, to foster in the minds of those waiting with him in the outpatients' clinic the impression that here was a man perhaps of some distinction. Why not play it for all it's worth? Otherwise it's defeat. His wife sat in a chair alongside him.

He would have preferred to have gone private, but couldn't afford it. He had been an operations manager for a contract catering company.

So, there he was, in his wheelchair, with prostate cancer, and the legs gone. Seventy-nine and his legs done for. Dressed up nicely, smartly. Striving to be a little different from the others who were waiting. Spoke quietly and pleasantly, with an assumption of authority. Played the game, as they used to say at his school.

'We're so sorry,' the receptionist in CT reception said. 'There's a wait of over an hour.'

He had nothing to read. Had brought nothing with which to divert himself. He sat there with a plastic cup of water. And the one hour became two, then three.

'We're so sorry. We have a malfunction with the scanner. We'll have to arrange an appointment on another day for you. We'll write.'

His wife wheeled him out to the lifts, down to ground floor. She phoned for a cab. They waited. Ten minutes. Then twenty until the cab came and took him home, where, exhausted by his visit to the hospital, by the effort he had made to appear urbane and notable, he was helped by his wife into his pyjamas. He sat before the television and turned on the cricket. It was the cricket that sustained him.

At half past six his wife came into the room.

THE LEGS AND THE DARK SUIT

There she went, her beautiful bare legs up and down in the all-round glass elevator in the modern retail and business building in the City of London. Several times every day she would ride the elevator between admin on the 5th and the fashion shops and restaurants on the Ground floor.

There was Randall; there he was behind the semi-circular bar inside Luca Roberto's Champagne Bar on the Ground floor. He was looking out as she went up and down, those beautiful long legs lightening his mornings, his afternoons.

There she was, pretending not to glance through the elevator glass at the guy, so smart in his dark suit, so narrow hipped, neatly put together. There she was, wondering, thinking, 'some guy'.

This was London, the City, rich and diverse, about its business. This is the story of the legs and the dark suit.

'Hi,' she said to him as she passed the open door of Luca Roberto's. 'Hi.'

He raised his hand in salutation. It was the beginning.

Later that day he stood at the open door of the bar as the elevator descended.

As she stepped out, she glanced over. She tried to assess his interest in her. She smiled and moved on.

When she came back, all she could see was his shadowy figure in the darkness of the interior.

She almost bumped into him on her way back from the Deli off Paternoster Square.

'Hi,' she said.

'Hi,' he said.

'Lunch,' she said, holding up a small green plastic bag. 'It's a nice day,' she said.

Sure, he said. It was.

'Lunch break,' she said.

'Sure,' he said.

'Well,' she said.

'Yeah,' he said.

Then he said: 'You have the most beautiful legs in the world.'

She was on the 5th floor. His beautiful smile, she thought. When he had smiled, it had been a gift. The smile on his face and in his dark eyes. It'd been his smile that did the trick, that filled her with a need to touch his face, to run her pale fingers down and across his cheek, to feel for his smoothly shaven stubble. But she did not.

Back down in the elevator she rode. He was standing at the door, not looking at her.

Returning, to go back to the 5th, she glanced, she tried not to glance, but glanced all the same, towards where he had been, but he was no longer there.

He wondered, as he dried a glass behind the bar in Luca Roberto's, did she shave between her legs? Did she wax strip? He hoped not. He wanted her to be a woman, not a pre-pubescent child.

An elderly couple came in. The elderly couple who had come in for salads and apple juices the week before. They chose to sit at the same table on the same padded seating. A retired couple. Summery. Educated. Pleasant. Long married, Randall surmised. The same salads as they had last time. Tap water. Bread. Apple juice for her. A small glass of red for him today.

Business was slow.

An American family, mother, father, teenage girl and younger boy entered, was seated. Cokes, burgers, salads. Mother and daughter withdrew into the safe exclusion of the internet and social media.

Randall checked on the elderly couple.

'We're fine.' the man said.

'Very nice, thank you,' the woman said of the cucumber, black olive and mint salad.

Randall walked to the door, looked out towards the elevator, then at the shoppers, the staff on their lunch breaks from Calvin Klein, Fraser Hart, Next, Oliver Bonas, the shopping bags, brief cases, summer outfits, high heels, shiny black shoes.

What was she doing?

She had small breasts. Small breasts were fine. Not too small, but discreet. Long legs, small breasts, long blonde hair to just below her suntanned shoulders. Her face. He couldn't at that moment quite remember her face, not in any detail. She was fair, had clear skin. Her eyes looking at him. His abdomen muscles tightening; he remembered that. Her eyes - blue-grey, were they?

He served the elderly man with a cappuccino. The American father payed the bill.

The waitress from the Ukraine checked in; part-time, four afternoons a week; dark hair, cool orange braces over her black top, clipped decoratively to the top of her black trousers. A cool lady. She had a boyfriend she lived with in Streatham. Streatham was well outside the City; another Country. Randall would never have visited Streatham. He'd heard of it, of course. He rented a flat in Old Street with two other guys. Three rooms, living room, kitchen, bathroom; small, expensive. OK for the City.

Thank you, and goodbye, the elderly couple said.

Randall smiled.

The Americans had left.

Two women in their forties at a table for two were sitting opposite each other drinking narrow flutes of champagne.

Two businessmen in shirtsleeves were at a table by the window near the door drinking Stella Artois.

Business was slow.

Randall took a break at three-thirty, took off for thirty minutes. Made his way to Festival Gardens, St Pauls, to sit, to take the weight off.

Did she have a boyfriend? Was she married? He hadn't looked for a ring.

And Joanne. What with Joanne? Joanne and him, cool relationship, uncommitted, that's how they liked it. Friday, Saturday nights; it was cool, just as it was.

The elevator woman, the legs; he realized he didn't know her name.

Luca Roberto's was closing, Randall was told. Business running at a loss. Closing 'with immediate effect'.

Randall stood outside the door of the bar, waiting for the elevator.

There she was, coming out of the elevator.

'Hi,' he said.

'Hi.'

'We've closed down.'

'Oh, no. Sorry.'

'Only -.'

'I'm meeting my bloke. Getting married in three weeks. It's all go,' she said.

'Congratulations.'

'Thanks. Nice meeting you. You're a sweet guy.'

'Thanks.'

'Really sweet. Sorry about Luca Roberto's.'

'Right.'

'You'll get a job easy.'

'Yep.'

'Well, bye.'

'Bye.'

He'd forgotten to ask her name.

There she went, her beautiful bare legs up and down in the all-round glass elevator in the City of London modern retail and business building. Every day, from the office on the 5th. As she got out at the Ground floor, she glanced over at Luca Roberto's; 'Closed for Business' printed on the card on the door, the interior as it had been; the tables, the semicircle bar, the optics, glasses. She wondered what had happened to the cool, classy-looking black guy. She would have liked to have known his name. It was his smile that did it. His dignity. His tall lean upright body. His serenity.

She would have liked to have met up with him again, but hadn't known where to start. She had regretted telling him she was getting married.

That was London. The City. On the move. The bit between its teeth. Dynamic. Transitory.

DENNY

Denny, at a distance, follows his old dad from Lotus Road, past the Conservative Association Club, Tesco's, and along Brackstone Road. He's calling out from time to time, not loudly.

'Dad,' he calls. Enough for the old man to hear, if he wants to.

The old man pushing his legs, best as he can nowadays, up the slight incline towards Rottingdene Road.

'Dad,' Denny, himself coming up to sixty, calls. 'Dad.'

The old man won't turn his head, but with fumbling keys enters the house, shuts the door behind him.

Denny outside, twenty-five metres off, standing, looking.

Denny not welcome. Not since his mother died all of a sudden. Lives in sheltered housing provided by Social Services.

'Wouldn't eat his bacon,' his father has said of him. 'Sits at the table, won't eat this, won't eat that, fusses. Doesn't work. Two jobs in more than forty-five years, two jobs lasting two weeks only.'

'Wouldn't eat his bacon,' he has said to the care worker.

The old man worked fifty years in steel. Never took a day off for sickness. Bought a BMW, like his workmates, Carl, Peter, Jack. Bought his house. Three bedrooms. Quiet neighbourhood. Snooker at the club, Tuesdays and Saturdays. The wife chatting with the wives near the bar. He doesn't play so much, not now.

Lost the knack. Denny, a grave disappointment. Lives on the 'Social'. Spends what he can get out of the old man, out of his mother when she was alive, at the bookies. Money like water. Doesn't lift a finger.

Denny stands looking at the house. Turns away now. Makes for the Rose and Crown. His mate Cristy could be at the Rose and Crown, lend Denny a few quid, stand him a pint.

Denny walking down Rottingdene Road.

'Dad,' he calls, quietly, not so as anyone can hear. He's not looking for trouble.

No one in the Rose and Crown, no one he knows. He waits. Slowly drinks a pint.

He walks to the Food Bank. Only, it's Wednesday, and the Food Bank opens Tuesdays and Fridays.

'Hello, Denny.'

The ladies are in the lounge of the sheltered housing where he lives. Always pleasant, although they know he's a scruff, with his unkempt beard. Could have been a nice looker, one of them thinks, had he pulled himself together, tidied himself up. Only, he can't help what he is, another one of them in there has said.

'Hello, Denny. You all right?'

'I'm all right,' Denny says.

'Been to the Food Bank?' one of them asks.

'It's not open, not till Friday,' another one says.

'It's not open till Friday,' says Denny.

'You're all right for food?' another one asks, hoping he won't ask for money. He's asked for money before. She gave him a couple of quid but she's not sure she ought to have. And since then she's not happy about giving him anymore. She doesn't want to encourage him. He's got to stand on his own feet. He has the 'Social', one of them has said.

He stands there in the lounge. The ladies, there are four of them, in the armchairs. The armchairs, they say, from the Heart Foundation. In good condition. No complaints. They look after you here. Jack, the warden, a very nice man. They all like him. Got a grandchild, he has. Girl. Jenny. Three years old. Denny has met her. Said, 'Hello.' 'Say hello to Jenny,' Jack has said to him. 'Hello, Jenny,' he said.

'Where are you off to now?' one of the four women asks.

They're all widows, the four of them. There are the heart problems, the arthritis, the fear of falling. Two of them have fallen, one in her bathroom, the other in the street outside Tesco's. It's nice here, it's safe. Any trouble and you pull the red cord or press the button hanging down from your neck. Press the button and someone comes looking for you. 'You all right?' they ask, and if not, it's the paramedics. They're a nice lot, the paras. God help us, what would we do without the paramedics, it's been said amongst them more than the once. And Jack the warden's nice. Got a three-year old granddaughter. Proud as punch he is. Nice man.

'So, where you off to, Denny?' one of them asks.

He doesn't know their names. He hasn't asked. He hasn't thought to ask. He doesn't think to ask. He likes them. They're OK. When he's asked by 'Social', by Jack, how he finds the ladies, he says they're OK. He smiles and says that, so Jack and 'Social' know he's OK, has no trouble with them. Thank God for them, for the ladies living here, at least he's got someone to chat to, a bit of life. Wandering about like he does, The Rose and Crown, the Food Bank, the bookies, for God's sake. They'll be no changing him there, Jack has said. 'Social' has had to accept the situation as it is. He's been spending his money, anything and everything he can get, on his gambling for God knows how many years. Decades it's been. There'll be no stopping him now.

'You seen your dad?' one of them asks.

'He's all right,' Denny says.

'Your dad all right, is he?'

'He had a turn.'

'Yes. He fell down, didn't he? In the High Street. He all right now, is he?'

'Yeah.'

He's going to go back to the Rose and Crown, see if Cristy is there. He's been told by Jack, not to ask for money from the residents here in sheltered housing. No asking for money, Denny, he was told. Told more than once. Several times, so he gets it into his head, like what he mustn't do. He'll go to the Rose, but he's got to make up his mind to move. He's standing in the lounge, as he knows. And the ladies been talking to him, asking after his dad, and he thinks he'll raise a hand now, and make for the outside door.

'See you later, Denny,' one and then another of the ladies says.

After he's gone one of the ladies says, 'His mother was cremated at the cemetery up by the bypass. The couple that own the Spar, near where Denny's dad lives, keep an eye open. When his dad's in there doing his shopping, they tell him if they've seen Denny hanging around.'

Denny is outside the house in Rottingdene Road.

Dad,' he calls. Loud enough for the old man to hear if he wants to. Although he thinks someone has said, the 'Social' perhaps, his dad is hard of hearing now, has lost his hearing. So, remembering, Denny tries again.

'Dad,' he calls. Louder. As loud as he can.

He watches for the net curtains in the front windows. Dad'll be in there, in the front room, unless he's in the kitchen. It'll be the front room or the kitchen. He waits for the net curtains to move.

He turns away. Makes it back along Rottingdene Road, past the Conservative Club.

The old man – his name's Ted – Ted's sure of that – it's Ted – he's got it. His name is Ted. He's in the kitchen with his lunch to make. Bit of smoked salmon he bought from Tesco's earlier. He walked down to Tesco's first thing. An early riser is Ted. Always has been. Has had to be. He doesn't hold with those who hang about in their beds. He's a man of habit. He's in the kitchen with the smoked salmon, and the bread, and the butter. He's making his sandwich. He's been out and bought the salmon and *The Daily Express*, and *The Times* for the crossword, because he's always bought *The Express*, and *The Times* for the crossword. He's bought *The Times* since he retired. God knows how long ago that was. He can't remember, can't be bothered to remember. He used to remember, used to be good at the crossword, only now he gets *The Times* so he can do the crossword, but he doesn't do it. Tried, sometimes tries, but it's got harder. He's eighty-seven. And he's had that fall, taken to A&E. In hospital for, God knows, he can't say how long. It must have been days. And now he's got the 'Social' come, help him out and thank God for that. He's grateful. Although it's a nuisance, an imposition. He never knows when they're coming. They keep the place clean, the washing. Otherwise, he can manage, thank you. He can make do on his own. He can't drive, not now. Not anymore, not since the fall. He's a prisoner in his own house, that's what he's said to the 'Social'. Said to the woman, who is a friend, she says, an old friend of him and his late wife, although he can't put a name to her, although he recognizes her when she comes, and she takes away his washing. He's making his lunch, smoked salmon, generous helping, bread, butter, a cup of tea. His son never lifted a finger. So, he'll manage very nicely as he is. With the salmon, the bread and butter, and a cup of tea, and *The Express* waiting for him in the front room, and *The Times* crossword. The tele is on the blink.

He's got his sandwich and his cup of tea now on the table by the armchair by the window in the front room. He's got *The Express*. Some idiot outside is shouting. He can't make it out. Can't be bothered. Got his sandwich, cup of tea. Got *The Express*. This used to be a nice neighbourhood.

Cristy isn't in the Rose. Denny'd go to the bookies, only he doesn't have the necessary. He hasn't got more than enough for half a pint, and he's saving that up for later, he tells himself.

'You want to make some money?' Denny imagines Cristy saying.

Cristy's not saying. Cristy's not come in the Rose. Only it's nice to think he's saying. It sort of keeps one going.

'I mean a lot of money. There's nothing to it, Denny,' Cristy's saying. 'All you got to do is stand outside Tesco's, five o'clock this afternoon – five o'clock,' he says, making it clear for Denny to understand, to get it into his head. 'Bloke comes over to you, asks for the way to the Scottish Highlands, Denny – don't worry about that – he says, 'Where's the Scottish Highlands?' and you say 'Half a pint, thank you'. You got that? He say, 'Where's the Scottish Highlands?' and you say to him in reply, 'Half a pint, thank you."

He has Denny repeat what he's told him. Denny repeats it, repeats it again and once again for good measure, for luck.

'He then hands you a carrier bag, Tesco's carrier bag. You take it, don't open it, don't look inside. If you want to look after yourself, don't look inside. Take it back to your room, in the housing.'

It's like in that movie thriller on the tele. One of them on the tele.

'You carry on just normal, like,' he hears Cristy saying. 'Till someone come and collect it. Right? Easy. No problem, Denny. You do that, and it's fifty quid. Fifty quid for you. The man or whoever come for the Tesco bag, he gives you fifty quid and then he hops it with the bag. Easy Denny.'

That's what Denny's imagining; Cristy coming in and Denny getting fifty quid for doing it. He'd seen it, something like it, on the tele. A movie.

Only, Cristy hasn't come in, and Denny's only got the ready cash for half a pint.

He goes to the bar, says to the barman, 'Half a pint, Fosters.'

'Right-oh, Denny,' the barman says.

It's half two. There's a lot more of the day to go.

The old man is washing up. The plate, the cup. Wiping down the surfaces. Making it neat and tidy, like always.

Denny's outside the house in Rottingdene Road, thinking of calling out.

THE BORDER

He was standing at the far-side of the out-of-town Tesco's car park. Waiting. He had been used to waiting. He was looking over towards the supermarket. He pulled about him his parka jacket against the raw north-easterly. He'd not worn the parka jacket in a long time. He scanned the parked cars, to see if he could see an Audi, Jane's car. He thought he could. He thought it was the red car, the bonnet jutting out from behind a silver Vauxhall Zafira.

That was her. She was there, coming over with two bags of shopping, her twice weekly shop, as he remembered. Wednesdays, she leaves the office, shops at the Tesco's. She was on her way over. He waved.

He called: 'Jane. Jane. Hello. It's me. Bernard.'

She had seen him. There she was. She was coming over with her bags.

'Hello, hello,' he called.

It was lovely to see her. Just like as ever. Five feet three. A tidy little number.

She was there. Standing there.

He said: 'Hello, my love, how are things with you?'

'Christ,' she said.

She put down her bags.

He said: 'Surprise, surprise!'

'Yes. It is,' she said.

'Remembered you do your weekend shopping, Tesco's on Wednesdays. I remembered.'

'Yes.'

She had known he was out. She'd told the kids. Dad would be back for Stacey's ninth birthday in November, she'd said. And Stacey thrilled, bouncing up and down. When could they see him, was he coming to live with them? And Max, thirteen and head of the family, knowing the situation. Well, Jane had said, he'd be living in Boreton. It'd be better that way and, of course, they'd be seeing him soon.

'It's ok. I'm on the right side of the line,' Bernard said to her. 'I'm in Boreton. I checked. Can't be too careful. Boreton finishes here, this side of Tesco's. You're in Braxton. I thought it'd be nice to see you. Sorry.'

'No. Only it's a bit strange – you there.'

'Got stuff in?'

'Yes.'

'So, what you planned for this evening, for the kids and you?'

'Oh. Shepherd's pie.'

'Very nice. Very nice. Tesco's shepherd's pie. Followed by hot chocolate fudge cake.'

'Well, maybe. I thought—'

'Whatever.'

Wing it. Sometimes you've got to extemporize. That was one of the things in this world he'd learnt. Like the border between Braxton and Boreton off the busy Braxton ring road. Not an exact clear-cut border, an approximation.

'It's good to be out,' he said now.

'I was expecting you to phone last night,' she said.

'Couldn't, could I? I hadn't got a phone. Not till this morning. New mobile – here we are,' he said. 'Pay as you go. Nothing fancy. No internet. Bernard here not permitted internet. What a load of crap, eh? What? Crap. Anyway, I've got it. Bought from the shop what's-it-called in Totley – this morning.'

It'd been four years.

She'd visited, once a month, driven out two and half hours there, two and a half back. Lined up, finger-printed, with the rest of them, families, mothers with their kids. They'd agreed about Max and Stacey not coming. Stacey was not ready for it. It'd not have been right. So, Jane had had to explain, had had to find the words, find a way of keeping a steady ship. John, their elder boy, had said he hadn't wanted to 'hang around'. He went off to Canada to be with his girlfriend.

She'd gone into the room. The prison officers seated on the raised platform. Some of the prisoners she had come to recognise. They and their visitors seated at plastic-top tables, with cups of tea, biscuits. Once a month, it'd been. Bernard there, standing, beaming, the big man, welcoming. He could welcome, could Bernard. He could put on the style. Had the larger-than-life charm. He could take one in, win one over. Everyone at the Constitution, at the Red Lion, in the shops in Braxton had loved Bernard. Heart and soul of the party, that's what they said. A good bloke. And not slow to buy a round. Although, God knows, a lot more than the once it was her round, him having prized the necessary out of her – 'Come on, girl, it's Friday, it's Saturday, it's Tuesday, it's been a hard week, twenty quid, I'm just a bit short on this particular occasion.'

There he was, in the prisoners' visitors' room, as if on duty; regulation blue and white stripe shirt, tie-up blue trousers; shoulders back, chest forward, the hand outstretched. The handshake fierce.

He was managing well, he said. He was 'counselling' inmates, a 'prison listener' he was called. There were some of them in there who had some stories to tell, he said, some lives they had led. Some couldn't write, could barely read, and this was the 21st century.

They always had a second cuppa from the refreshment counter. And a piece of cake, and a Kit Kat. The Kit Kat for later, he said. He said, always said, let him pay. No, she said, she'd pay. Well, thanks, very kind, he always said. Very kind. Which made her want to cry. My turn next time around, he said. He always asked about the kids, about Lucy who was baby-sitting Stacey. The kids were doing well at school, she'd say. She didn't tell him Stacey was getting behind with her schoolwork.

'I don't want to keep you,' he said. 'You got to get back to the kids. Back from school now, eh? Lucy looking after them? Good old Lucy. We go back a long way, eh? Her and bastard Gerald. The bastard walking out on her with that woman, opening a bar in Malaga, for Christ's sake. The Constitution Club – you, me, Lucy, Gerald – Friday nights, the snooker, the camaraderie, then the bastard buggers off. You go there still, you and Lucy now?

'No.'

'You and Lucy?'

'We go to the White Horse.'

'Yeah. You said. It's the White Horse now. Faithful, loyal, that's Lucy – we're lucky to have her. How's her dad?'

'He just watches the tele all day.'

'Parkinson's. Yeah,' he said. 'Poor Lucy. Never got over Gerald – buggering off with that woman to Malaga or wherever it was. That didn't last long, she didn't last long, did she?'

'How's the flat?' she asked.

'Oh, oh, yes, very nice. Well, not anything palatial, you understand. Bed-sit, kitchen, bathroom. Beggars can't be choosers and all that – grateful for small mercies, eh? The landlord seems all right – Greek – but there you go. Eh? Beggars, as I say. Do for the time being. Get myself settled. I've got a few possibilities, a few ideas, you know, as ever. I was very much hoping I could have a dog, but the landlord says he doesn't allow it. So, there we have it, eh?'

A dog. If Maisie was alive. Maisie, his black Labrador. It'd have been all right with her. The two of them together. She'd passed away, Jane told him when she visited. It broke his heart, set him back that did – had shed tears for the loss of Maisie. The kids at the Children's Home had loved her. The little blighters, all that energy, cooped up inside. He'd get them out with the dog, with Maisie, in the field at the back. Them playing footer, running about, that was the thing, that was what they needed. That lad – what-was-his-name? – wouldn't do anything, kept himself to himself, miserable. He takes the dog over. 'Give him a stroke, lad, she's lovely,' he told the boy. The lad and Maisie, they become mates, the lad transformed. Everyone needs a dog, Bernard had said. Everyone needs a fucking dog, he had cried out after he heard she'd died, and again after the landlord had gone and had said no dogs. They loved Maisie, those kids, she was a star. I could fuck off, he'd said to the Children's Home inspectors. They don't need me, not when they've got the dog. He was joking, of course. He had to explain to the inspectors it was a joke. God help them.

'No, the flat will do until something better comes along,' he said. 'What about you, Jane, my love – work going well, is it?'

'It's all right. Busy,' she said.

'Whenever was it not?' he said. 'You're going to go to the very top, my love – oh, yes – always said so, didn't I? – always said you had what it takes – social services, just your kettle of fish, no doubt about it. I always said, didn't I?'

She thought him so brave. Standing there, putting on a front, looking on the bright side. That was Bernard. Not giving up. Bouncing back. Just a small miscalculation, he'd say when things went wrong. Nothing that can't be put right, he'd say. Always the same. And the dog, Maisie, he loved her. Him and Max over at the recreation ground. Playing football. Five-year old Max running rings round him, Bernard making a show, a big act of failing to get the ball off him. Max the champion. Max going to be signed up for Manchester City. And the dog running about, one of the family.

'You all right for money?' she asked him.

'Yeah. I'll make do. As ever.'

'I can let you have some.'

'I'm all right. I'd only spend it on the GG's.'

Old joke. The stock answer.

'You've been to see your mum?' she said.

'Oh, yeah,' he said. 'I went down there, saw her in the Nursing Home. Very nice, nice place, I thought. Went straight down there. Thought, well, better than coming up here and then having to go all the way down there after. She's all right. Well cared for. She not say much, to be frank. The doctors say they don't think she's got long. It's more than likely she'll not last out much beyond Christmas.

Ninety-three. I said to her, you know, I'd been away, business, overseas. I was telling her, reminded her, about how we, her, dad and me, used to go to Tenby – holidays.'

He had walked the half mile and more from the railway station. No cabs about. He'd asked the man in the ticket office for the directions to the Nursing Home. Up along the main road, the man told him, past the playing fields. Turn left at the Rose and Anchor.

'It's just along from there,' the man had said. 'About a mile.'

'Thank you very much, sir,' he said. 'Much obliged to you.'

Courtesy was the byword. Affability. Gets one a long way does affability and a courteous manner, that was his belief.

It was further than he had been given to believe. Quite a bit more than a mile in his estimation. It was his knees that were the bother. He popped into the Rose and Crown for a quick pint.

No tele on, which was a blessing. No music. A few customers. Regulars by the look of them.

'A pint of your very best, if you'd be so kind,' he said to the barman with tattoos on his arms.

It was everywhere now, tattoos. Women too, despoiling their natural looks, the younger ones. God help us, he thought, what did they think they would look like when they were old, when they were his age, for God's sake, when they were in their late sixties. He'd seen that woman outside the station, in her fifties probably, obese, a tattoo right across her half-exposed breasts. Couldn't make out what it said. Right across the top of her breasts. It was a shock.

'It's a bit of a haul up from the station, isn't it?' he said to a man in a brown sports jacket standing at the bar just down from him.

'Right,' the man said shortly. He was not one to share the time of day, that was apparent.

'No cabs about,' Bernard said. Not complaining, just making conversation. Camaraderie. Not enough of that in the world today.

'There's a mini cab number at the side of the bar.' This said by a woman, nicely turned out, in her sixties or more, sitting by a gent, under the window overlooking the empty street.

'Thanks very much. Much obliged. I'll make a note of it. Just off to the Nursing Home – my old mother, bless her.'

'She'll be pleased to see you,' the woman under the window said.

He decided he'd have another quick pint.

He was in his mother's room in the Nursing Home. The curtains half drawn against the light. His mother, shrunken, beneath the bedclothes. This woman who had always prided herself on her dress sense, her stylish and elegant outfits. A tough and determined woman. Her face now in shadow.

'Hello, Mum.'

He lent down, gave her a kiss on her forehead. He thought she smiled. He drew up a chair, sat by the bedside. His knees hurt. It was always his knees.

'I'm sorry I've not been to see you for quite a while, Mum. Only, I've been away. Africa – working with an Oxfam type outfit.'

You tell one lie. Then another. It becomes a way of life.

'I've just seen the nurse. She says you're doing very well, all told. She seems very nice, doesn't she?'

He shifted his position in the upright chair. It was too small for him. Not big enough.

'You got my cards, did you?' he said. 'My Christmas and birthday cards? I'm sorry, I had to send them to you through Jane – only I wasn't sure that you were at the same Nursing Home – I thought it safer. You got them all right, did you? There's not much of a postal service where I was. I mean, I'm there in the middle of darkest Africa, can't phone, no mobile connection – you can imagine.'

He'd not seen her in all the four years. He'd asked Jane to tell her he had had to go abroad, working for the Charity. She wouldn't have wanted to know the truth. You'd not do that to an old woman, not to her.

He shifted himself.

'Jane told me you got a bit of pneumonia last Christmas. Blimey, that can't have been nice, not at all, not one little bit. I am sorry to hear that. But, anyway, you're better now, aren't you? The nurse here tells me you're doing all right. She says you're tough, you're a tough one, she says. Well, we all know that, don't we? You always have been, eh? You're a fighter. That's my mum. A fighter. 'An irresistible force', that's what Dad used to say about you. 'An irresistible force, that's your mother,' he used to say, eh? He's right too and make no mistake. No truer word.'

He had to shift himself again, make himself comfortable. He didn't rightly know if she was looking at him, not properly. He could have done with another pint.

'It's a bit of a hike getting down here, isn't it? Took me all of two hours and more. But there we go. Jane and the kids send their love. Jane came to see you in September, didn't she? She and the kids are fine, fine and dandy. Max and Stacey, they're doing very well – no doubt about it. None at all. You should see Max playing football, he's a marvel at football. He's doing very well with his school work too – he's brainy – takes after his mother. Not after me, that's for sure. Takes after Dad. And Jane's in line for another promotion, I reckon.'

Think of good things. The cruise she went on with Dad. He reminded her. The Canaries, Lanzarote, Madeira, very stylish. Family holidays when he was a kid in Tenby. They'd hired bikes. The fish and chips.

'And John, our son John,' he said. 'He's out in Canada, Mum. He's out there, him and his Canadian girlfriend. Works in computers. Another brainy member of the family. Miss him, of course. You remember you and Dad taking him to the Isle of Wight that time, he had a wonderful time, you and John – he was the apple of your eye. Those holidays he spent with you, wonderful. He never stopped talking about it, I remember. I reckon Jane and I ought to take Stacey and Max to the Isle of Wight. Me and Jane, take them both to the Isle of Wight – come back, tell you if it's changed at all in any way.'

Keep going. One had to keep going. Couldn't sit there, saying nothing.

The nurse came in with his mother's meds. A black woman, Nigerian by the looks of her, he thought. The jolly sort. Stroked Mum's forehead. Called her 'darling'. 'You all right, darling? Your son's here. Here to see you, darling. That's nice, isn't it?'

On his walk back to the station, he popped into the Rose and Crown. He could catch the six ten, get into Boreton just after half seven, get something to eat at the pub near the station or in a café.

'Do you serve food?' he said to the young woman behind the bar.

'Crisps,' she said.

She was about thirty, he reckoned. Thirty. Probably married. Or a single mum – her friend or mother looking after the kid – baby-sitting. Baby-sitting, that was the thing – him baby-sitting

Max when he was little, and then Stacey when Jane went off to her classes, upping her qualifications and good on her. Don't say he ever stood in her way, on the contrary. Always encouraged her. Get on with it, girl, he used to say. You'll be at the top of your profession, top of the tree one day, no doubt about it.

'Another one in there, if you please, Miss.'

Him old-fashioned, the way he speaks – people liked that. 'Posh', that's what the lads inside said. No hard feelings. Got on very well with them. Miss them, if truth be told. He'd not say no if he was to meet some of them outside. That Terry, he was a good man. Owned the car hire firm. Family business. We'll meet again, they said. Like the Vera Lynn song, they'd said – like the Vera Lynn. "We'll meet again, don't know where, don't know when—"

'Sorry about that,' he said to the barmaid. 'The singing – quite forgot myself.'

He'd upset her now. The way she didn't reply. The way she just looked, then turned her attention to the far side of the bar.

The lights from Tesco's seemed brighter now against the darkening sky.

'You need any money?' Jane asked again.

'No.'

'I can let you have some.'

'I'm all right. No bother.'

It was the drink, the too-long stay in the Mason's Arms outside Braxton that time. Back at the Children's Home, the tentative touch of her contemptuously proffered breast through the thin white cotton of her top. Fifteen years old. And twenty-five years later she and her friends make their move. After the Court case, them out there in the corridor, where's the money? they're shouting, where's the money?

'How's Alan?' he asked Jane.

'Yes, he's all right,' she said.

'Good man Alan, from the sound of him – from what you say. Quantity Surveyor.'

'Project Manager.'

'Project manager, that's right. I remember you saying. Very nice. Construction industry, you said. You've got a good man there. Solid. Dependable. You look good, better than ever. You and Alan, that's fine, fine.'

She'd told him about Alan that time she visited him in prison. Said she'd met him through Lucy. Lucy and Alan were going out – nothing serious – then it was Alan and Jane going out.

He was happy for her, Bernard said.

'The Hare and Hounds, Cleethley – we could meet, have a drink tomorrow or sometime, Cleethley's no problem,' he said.

'I'll have to ask Lucy. See if she can babysit,' she said.

'That's it. Good old Lucy, eh?'

She wouldn't tell him about the complaints to the Centre, about 'Paedos Welcome Here' scrawled on the Centre's front wall. About the parents at Stacey's school, worried for the safety of their kids. Bernard didn't know about that. No good telling him. No good telling him she was thinking of applying for a job down South. She had not told Lucy – it would have broken her heart.

'Tea at the George Hotel, you, me, the kids,' he said. 'We talked about it. Can't see no harm in that.'

'Oh. Yes,' she said.

'I'll check it out with the powers-that-be. The police.'

He had to make sure he wasn't contravening the rules. He had to keep them apprised of his movements. No going down Tankerton Road near the infants' school. What he was supposed to do to anyone in or about the infant's school he hadn't a clue. But no, Tankerton Road was out of bounds.

'I'll make the appropriate enquiries,' he said. 'Make sure The George is OK. Get the thumbs up. Once I've got settled, found my feet, you know – got the act together so to speak, see where I am, where I stand, I'm thinking I'll try and get some work, barman or something. Got a bloke down in Whitestone, you remember him? Dick, with the garage. I was thinking maybe I – I was thinking I'll give him a buzz, pop over, have a word, see if he has anything – reception, a couple of hours or so. And I got this friend of mine, Terry – I told you about Terry – a bloke with me inside – he was done for – well, anyway, he's coming out just before Christmas. He's got a car hire firm, Bournemouth – or rather he had, he had. Anyway, he's not too badly off if you take my meaning. He's got a bit put aside, talking about setting up a business again, said him and me – we could start something up.'

'Good.'

'Yeah. Got to look on the bright side, eh? I did my best with those kids you know.

'I know.'

'Hey, what about that kid Thomas! He was in the Home that last year I was there – a right handful – senior manager at Lowson Electrics now.'

Jane's phone buzzed

'Everything all right?' he asked.

'It's Lucy,' she said.

'Best get going. The kids' dinner. Eh? Don't want to keep them waiting, do we?'

'No.'

'I'm thinking I'll go over to Canada. Go and see our John. He has never been one for sitting around, has he? Bit like his dad. He wrote, said that I'll be welcome, more than welcome, come over and stay. Got a nice big flat, with his girl-friend, Judy. Well, listen to me, I don't have to tell you that, eh? Come over, he says. I'll get permission, try and get permission, can't see why not. What am I going to do over there? John, he can vouch for me, tell them he'll keep a check on me, or whatever it is they bloody want of me, like I'm some sort of maniac. I'll get permission, try to get permission. Very nice. Always wanted to go to Canada. Better standard of living. Just a visit. Holiday. Three or four weeks. I'm going to see about it, about going over to see John in Canada, make enquiries.'

'Yes. I better go – sorry.'

'No, no. You get yourself home. It's good to be out, eh?'

'Yes, yes.'

She picked up her bags and turned to go.

'Hare and Hounds, Cleethley tomorrow, let me know, eh?' he called. 'See what we can do about The George on Saturday. See what we can arrange.'

'Take care,' she said.

'Yes, rather. No worries on that score. No, none at all.'

He watched her now as she made her way to her Audi.

He was looking as the red car pulled out of the car park, and joined the rush hour traffic on the busy Braxton ring road.

THE SHOOT

The owner of the hotel, a woman in her thirties, came to their table. Held herself erect. Presented herself with a fixed smile.

'Is everything all right?' she asked. Pleasant enough.

'Thank you,' one of their number replied.

They were part of a television crew, shooting a commercial for Fiat in the grounds of an old house in the County of Wexford.

The woman smiled pleasantly.

'Can we have another bottle of the red wine please?' Sparks said.

Her smile retreated. She swayed.

'Of course,' she said.

She retreated to the far end of the long dining room and into the kitchen. Did so, one deliberate step after the other, self-consciously maintaining her erect posture.

'She's pissed,' the young runner, who had the nickname 'Odd-Jobs', said to Sparks.

The next morning as they were leaving to set up for the shoot, the woman was in the narrow reception area. Huddled against the harshness of the day. In an off-white dressing gown. Her hair astray.

In the coach that was to take them up the coast, Sparks said, 'Her husband was killed in Afghanistan.'

The last day of the shoot. Before breakfast, Sparks and Odd-Jobs walked the short distance down to the shore. Looked across the calm flat sea, sparkling in the early morning sun like a million diamonds.

OUR REVELS NOW ARE ENDED

From early dawn to sunset Len could be found by the lake and in the grassland and secluded woodland of the park. He was a gardener there for over twenty-five years. The lakeside where he worked, clearing litter, making good overnight-damage, planting out and pruning, was his province and his pride. It was his domain.

Those who visited the lakeside would observe the gaunt figure of Len with his spade and fork, his solitariness, his singularity. His limbs were long and narrow, his arms were skin and muscle. He had not an inch of fat upon him. His face was craggy. Deep lines ran down from the sides of his nose to his chin. His jaw line was a sheer cliff of bone. He walked with a long step. He did not linger without intention.

He was at one with the nesting Herons and Cormorants, with the Tawny Owl, the Green Woodpecker and Kestrel. He oversaw the regal lettuce loving Mute Swan, the common Mallard, the native Greylag Geese, the exotic Mandarin, the Moorhen and the Tufted Duck. Within his realm were the winter-feeding Chaffinch, the sleepless Blackbird, the melodious Great Tit, the snail cracking Song Thrush and the fecund Crow. He followed and noted the movement of birds flying from south-west to north-east in the spring, and north-east to south-west in the autumn. He knew where to find the common Frog, the smooth Newt, the Dragonflies, the Fox, the Brown Rat, the Grey Squirrel and the shy Hedgehog. The wildlife loggeries and dead hedges, the wetland and wildflowers of the Silt Pen were within his jurisdiction. These were his subjects, his companions.

He was acquainted with the visitors to the park, the dog walkers, the mothers and children, nannies, lovers, adulterers, the drunken, the drug addicts, the homeless, men lingering. He did not happily tolerate those who abandoned their sweet papers, their cartons, cans and bottles on the grass, on the flowerbeds, the shrubbery and herbaceous borders. His polite yet persistent requests that rubbish should be put in the waste bins were met by some with incredulity that a lowly gardener would speak to them at all, let alone make such demands of them. He said it mattered not to him whether the offenders were British, Chinese or American, Russian, Ethiopian, Italian or Somali. When it came to litter, he expected it to be picked up and deposited by the owner in the appropriate place.

He could be seen at noontide to walk to his shed, his cell, where he had his midday meal, his home-made sandwich, his apple, a bottle of tap water. On the makeshift table before him were biographies of the great theatre stars of the past, of Olivier, Gielgud, Richardson, Irving, Terry, and the Complete Works of William Shakespeare. His favourite character was Prospero. He liked to read the verse aloud, and expertly, paying heed to the iambic pentameters. For, in his younger days, he had been an actor.

At the end of the day he would put away his tools, the 'instruments' of his trade and calling.

The first sign that there was something wrong was when, one evening, he found himself lost while trying to get home. He told himself he must have been dreaming. It was out of character.

Later he forgot the names of the Chaffinch, the Greylag Geese, the Pied Wagtail, the Knapweed and Meadow Crane's Bill. He had to struggle to remember them. It bothered him.

The day came when, returning home from work, he had stood helpless before his front door unable to work out how he was to open it. He stared at it, at the door frame, at the keyhole. His hand went to his pocket and he took out the key. But the relationship between key and keyhole was beyond him, was outside his understanding. He had lost his magic.

On retiring, his friends in London wondered where he was, and he, for his part, had forgotten them and within a year all memory had disappeared, of the waterside, the waterfowl, the flora and fauna, the Shakespearean verse, of Prospero, Hamlet, Macbeth, Angelo, of Ariel and Miranda. All had melted into thin air, leaving not a rack behind, until, as he lay in hospital, with a nurse holding his hand in hers, it was discovered he had forgotten how to swallow, and then to breathe.

Recalling him, it was surmised by jovial loving friends that the soul of this man, with his boyish smile and enthusiasm, his light laugh and shy welcome, had flown to Heaven where he was joined by the Almighty and His angels as he patiently attempted to explain to them the natural wonders of the iambic pentameter and the magic and beauty of the planet Earth.

THE SQUARE

1968. From the third-floor front window of the flat where the girls lived Aretha Franklin singing 'Say A Little Prayer' filled all corners of the square. The girls – young women – were Julie and Becky, nurses. Saturday morning. Midsummer. Their day off. The song a declaration, an announcement to the world beyond their windows of the joy of being at leisure, of being alive.

Aretha Franklin's 'Say A Little Prayer' backed by The Sweet Inspirations rang out loud and clear and vigorous across the square, sweeping through and among the verdant plane trees, reaching every front door, front room, every side entrance as Becky before the bathroom mirror, hair washed and wet, held her full breasts in her hands, lifted them, let them drop, lifted them, let them drop. She put on her deodorant, sang along, going out as she was with a boy she didn't know, had only met the once, but he had seemed all right, nice face, bit spotty, lovely smile. It was the smile that did it, had her say yes, ok, Saturday 7.30. The Queen's Head.

Julie danced to Aretha's 'Night Time Is the Right Time' and, looking out of the window across the square, saw old Mr what's-his-name – Dunstan, that was it – returning from the corner shop, and him thinking 'good to hear the music again this Saturday,' and waving up at the girl in the window, before returning to his rented accommodation, the basement flat in the house on the corner.

Aretha's powerful voice reached the ears of the young man from 'up north' who, in the front room of the ground floor flat across the square from Julie and Becky's building, was writing his first stage play. Had young Becky and Julie known more of the young man – his name was Brian – known of his potential for fame and fortune, his future eminence, well, then, Becky and Julie might well have gone out of their way to acquaint themselves with him, though he hadn't seemed quite their type, he being rather fusty in appearance, rather intellectual, shy, with spectacles. 'Quite a sweet face. A gentle person,' Becky thought as she dried her dark hair. But she and Julie had said the man, whose name they had thought was Brian, was not really their type, he wasn't the sort to go in for dancing.

'He's too bookish,' Julie thought, while choosing her outfit for her Saturday night at the disco club with nurses Samantha and Jane.

Brian in his front room liked to hear Aretha, the usual Saturday morning concert, as he thought of it. He, in his way, considered Aretha's voice uplifting. At that time, that moment in time, sitting there with the first draft of the first act of his first play on the table before him, he felt obliged to admit to himself that, all in all, he could himself do with a bit of an uplift, a bit of a perk up, someone to love, someone to fill a hole so to speak. It was lonely, writing. He'd go out for a walk but then he'd only have to come back again and stare at the first draft. A cup of coffee might do the trick, raise his spirits. On the other hand, he'd already had three cups of coffee that morning, and they did say, he was sure he'd read it in the newspaper, *The Guardian*, that too much coffee was bad for one, for the heart. Life, he had decided, was hazardous. He'd seen the girls up at the window, leaning out. He had seen them from time to time on those occasions when he'd returned from the corner shop where he went for his eggs and beans and bread and *The Guardian* and *The Telegraph*, and he had thought them very young, like himself. He had thought them to be very lively, which, he felt, was not especially like himself. They were extrovert types, and he envied them. How nice to be them, how wonderful not to have to sit down and try to write the first draft of one's first play. Once he'd finished this play, he thought, he'd chuck it in, give it up, become like the two girls across the square, play loud music, dance, dry his hair while standing for all the world to see at the open window. In the meantime, he decided, he'd have another cup of coffee.

Becky and Julie, leaning out of the window, observed the tall fellow, the one with the beard, striding across the square towards the street leading to the main road. In the pause between Aretha's *'Darling, You Send Me'* and *'You're A Sweet, Sweet Man'*, they heard him whistling in imitation of a ringing telephone. Persistently he whistled the ringing, again and again. And again. Head forward, intent. This was Mark. A television producer. Becky and Julie had watched him one afternoon whistling his way to his basement flat in the building across from theirs and two doors from the writer Brian. People said he was dabbling in magic mushrooms and LSD. He had begun to believe that God was urging him onward, that, through the use of the drugs, he was part of a worldwide governmental attempt to secure a common state of world peace. This was 1968. Such beliefs were possible.

In the ground-floor flat of Becky and Julie's building Peter was shouting. He was trying all he could to persuade his wife Rachel not to leave him. But Rachel had had enough of his depression, his shouting, his unemployment, his smoking, everything. And he had fucked that girl from the pub where he played his guitar. And Rachel with the new baby couldn't cope. She'd had enough. She was going away to her sister's, at least for a while, then she'd see how things were, but frankly, Peter, it was no good, she couldn't stand it. If truth were told, in her opinion, Peter was a selfish, self-regarding neurotic, and though she loved him, he had failed the test, lost the opportunity, she was leaving him. And he was shouting. Shouting so loudly that neither he nor Rachel could hear Aretha belting out '*I Take What I Want*'.

As Julie and Becky drew back from the window, as the writer Brian drank his coffee before returning to the first act draft, as old Mr Dunstan in his basement continued to put away his groceries, the piece of cheese, the bread, the milk, the tin of tuna, the fairy cakes, as whistling TV producer Mark walked towards the bridge that led to the tube station and saw an eagle with angel's wings soaring across a purple sky, Rachel, in desperation, threw a glass at shouting Peter which missed, as intended, and smashed against the living room wall.

Well past midnight, Julie was out with Samantha and Jane dancing their socks off at the disco, getting a 'wee-bit-tight, girls', with no bloke in sight they fancied, more girls there than men – but who cares. Dancing was what they were there for and dancing they did, and did, and did, and no thought for Sunday morning, waking with the headache, the taste in the mouth, the long lie-in.

Becky was at home, in her dressing gown, with a cup of hot chocolate, didn't stay out, not with that chap, nice enough, but he was too persistent. She wasn't going to take him in her mouth, why should she? She didn't do that, not take a man's cock in her mouth, not Becky, not till she was ready to do it, and to her way of thinking it would be with a husband, with the father of her children. That was Becky. A man, with spots, who kept on and on about him wanting her to put his cock in her mouth was not her kettle of fish, her choice of partner, not her type at all. So, it was hot chocolate. It was Aretha now, 'I Can't See Myself Leaving You', playing softly, and Becky thinking she might phone her mum although it was too late, she'd be asleep, so she wouldn't, though she'd have liked to. But it was ok. She was ok. Nice hot chocolate. And there was Aretha.

Mark the TV producer was unconscious in a police cell, a doctor in attendance, an ambulance called.

Young northern writer Brian was in bed, his hand on the job, masturbating being a nice way of getting to sleep.

Mr Dunstan was walking up and down his bedroom for lying down hurt his legs.

Rachel had packed an overnight bag, had scooped up the baby, their baby, and had taken a taxi to her sister Carol's without telling Peter where she was going.

And Peter was shouting.

Sunday morning. Sun shining. Another lovely day. The square open, clear, serene. Still. Eleven o'clock. No Aretha now. Julie asleep. Becky, washing her hair, admiring her breasts in the bathroom mirror, waiting for motherhood.

Old Mr Dunstan dead – old age – heart failure – waiting to be discovered on Monday by the care worker.

Writer Brian with a cup of coffee, flipping through the first draft of the first act, thinking he'd phone a friend, Jason, meet for lunch at that café, ordinary café, with real people there, roast beef, or lamb, yes, he'd phone Jason.

Peter limping towards Camden, towards he-did-not-know-where, in a daze.

In his and Rachel's flat, the walls of the living room, of the bedroom, of the bathroom and kitchen sprayed in red 'Peter Loves Rachel'.

Becky at the window on the third floor, looking out at the empty square, seeing everywhere, 'Peter Loves Rachel' in red – on the walls, the pavements, the road, the side of a building and as far as her eyes could see.

2014. Becky sits in her garden in Somerset. It's Saturday morning. Her children Louis and Carla are coming, along with Louis' wife Sarah and their boys Malcolm and Derrick, and their dog Bonzo.

Richard, her husband for forty-one years, died in 2011. Heart attack. Sudden. No warning. The thief in the night, someone said, although he died at 11.37 on a Saturday morning.

She has a lovely garden, the apple tree, the green, green lawn. She's retired now. Worked in the NHS for thirty-seven years, other than when the children were little. Rheumatology specialist nurse.

She's still in touch with Julie who lives in Canada. Facebook. Both on Facebook. And Skype. All praises to Skype. Julie married, the second time around, a Canadian journalist, Morris. They adopted a girl, little Cindy, who of course is now a woman.

The last time Becky spoke to Julie on Skype she told Julie that – wonderful news – Rachel and Peter were back together again. She had read an article about record shops in the UK and there was this one in Wales, in Barmouth, and it's owned by Peter and Rachel. Vintage, vinyl stuff, 45's, LPs, wind up gramophones, Magnovox console stereos. Becky had written to them that it was lovely to read about them and about their shop and they both looked, in the photo in the paper, so young – and did they remember Julie and her, top floor, in the square, late sixties? And, guess what, Becky had told Julie, Rachel replied and sent Becky the 1968 *'Aretha Now'* album. Rachel wrote that she and Peter had been together again since 1974 and their son Toby worked for the Council and was married with four kids. She wrote that Peter had had a breakdown when they were living in the square, but he came through it. She had always loved him. They loved it in Wales, at Barmouth, and on Sundays she and Peter walked the long beach all the six miles to the village of Tal-y-Bont. The beach, Rachel wrote, is within a Site of Special Scientific Interest and next to the National Nature Reserve, and there are lovely walks to be had along the coast and the people in the area are so friendly and helpful. 'Well, it's a community, Becky,' she wrote. 'On a Saturday night everyone in the village gets down to the pub, has a bit of a sing song, a few pints. They like their beer, do the Welsh. And the shop is really popular, which is a bit of a surprise, money being short, what with the economy, the state of the country, the unemployment.' But they kept going and Rachel herself was working part-time for a housing association. If Becky was ever thinking of having a holiday, she'd not be disappointed with Barmouth, it'd be lovely to see her, and they'd love to see Julie too of course if she ever decided to come back to England sometime for a holiday. And the letter went on, the letter that came with the album, twelve pages of it.

Every morning Mark, the one-time television producer, plays a penny whistle in the underpass at Marble Arch.

Midday Saturday morning. Becky's son Louis and his wife Sarah and their boys Malcolm and Derrick, and Becky's daughter Carla have arrived. The boys are in the garden, playing French cricket with their father. Sarah is in the kitchen preparing a special salad she insists on making. Becky is upstairs in the bathroom, grieving for Richard. It is always the same when the children visit. No Richard, no Richard to share the day. Dr Richard Dobson, junior doctor, later to be a consultant paediatrician at the London Hospital. 'Hiya,' he used to call as she, Nurse Becky Leatherby, passed by. 'Hiya, Becky,' he calls, that grin, the cheeky bugger, that mop of black hair, 'you fancy a drink, Saturday,' he says. It's the rugby club, in the bar, after his game. All those sweaty hearty men, the beer flowing, the laughter, the testosterone. A year later they were married. And now the cheeky bugger has fucked off. Gone and left her. On the squash court, showing off, playing a man almost half his age, heart attack, sudden collapse, dead. Gone. The cheeky fucking bugger. She quietly weeps, weeps too for her left breast. Lost to cancer.

In Toronto Julie is clearing up after breakfast. Morris, her Canadian, is over at his friend Baxter's place working on his 1949 Packard Super 8 Sedan. This evening Julie and Morris will go dancing. They are members of the local dance group who meet on Saturday evenings in the Community Centre at St Michael's Anglican Church. From time to time, when the mood takes them, they dance together late at night in their living room, their arms around each other. She likes that. Morris is her second husband. Julie's first husband was an alcoholic. Their adopted daughter Cindy has a good job in the Mayor's Office. No partner. Not just yet. Is happy. Brainy. 'Doesn't get it from me,' Julie has said to Becky. Every time Cindy comes up in conversation during their phone calls Julie says, 'Cindy is brainy – she doesn't get it from me.'

It's Saturday morning. Brian is back home in Gloucestershire. The Writers' Guild Award, bestowed on him last night for his outstanding contribution to writing and writers, sits on a shelf in the airing cupboard 'with the rest of them'. Jason is in their small garden picking peas. It's halibut for lunch. Halibut with a pea and onion salad. Brian likes halibut. The very name itself. So unpretentious. He thinks to himself, comfortably seated in his plaid-upholstered armchair in earth shades from Colefax and Fowler with *The Saturday Guardian* on his lap, that halibut might well feature in some way or other in his next play, which may or may not, he thinks, be about C.S. Lewis and J.R.R. Tolkien. And in view of the latest award he has received, he thinks a glass of white wine might well be in order. A Chardonnay or a Sauvignon Blanc.

After Becky's family has gone home, she Skypes Julie. They observe each other's faces on their screens.

Julie says, 'Have you had a nice day?'

Becky says, 'Yes, it's lovely having them here.'

'My screen,' Julie says. 'You look all red.'

'I've been in the sun,' Becky says.

'No, it's the screen, the camera, I'm sure it's the camera,' Julie says.

'You look fine,' Becky says. 'Nice and clear.'

'Hey,' Julie says, with, at that moment, nothing else to say. 'You remember the disco in Parkway? Hey, bet it's not there now.'

Becky says, 'No, I don't suppose it is.'

'Do you ever feel left behind?' Julie says.

'What do you mean?' Becky says.

'I don't know,' Julie says. And she doesn't. It is just a feeling she has.

They talk family, talk health, talk about Becky's lost left breast. Talk about their husbands, Richard and Morris, their kids, grandchildren. They say some of the same things they did the last time they spoke, but that's ok, it's the sound you make, that's what it's about. It's the sound. That's what Julie has read, and whoever wrote that was right, dead right. And from time to time during these transatlantic Skype calls and again this Saturday evening Julie weeps for Becky's breast lost to cancer and her loss of her Richard who, as Julie remembers, was such a nice, nice man.

'Don't cry, Julie dear,' Becky says, seeing the tears in her eyes, tears now rolling down her cheeks. 'Don't cry.'

'I'm always praying for you, Becky darling,' Julie says – she's always saying that.

And later, after their phone call, the thought of Richard and of Becky will start her off again, the tears welling up, although she doesn't know why she does it, but she's doing it again, until Morris comes in the bedroom and says, 'What's up?' And she says, 'It's Becky, just Becky, her cancer and her husband Richard,' and Morris nods the way he does, all that grey hair, so much hair on that head, and he says, 'Yep.' That's all. It's enough. 'Yep.'

'The halibut was very nice,' Brian says to Jason. He's said it before; he says it again. 'Very nice, the halibut.'

'Do you think we should get married?' he says to Jason.

'I thought you'd never ask,' Jason says.

'Something quiet, private,' Brian says. 'Between ourselves.'

'And Buddy, Ros, Michael and – and Sarah and Bill,' says Jason.

'No more, just them,' says Brian.

It's Saturday evening, they are in the garden, Brian with *The Saturday Guardian*, Jason with a potted plant.

'It's a geranium,' Jason says.

'I thought it was a geranium,' Brian says.

He watches Jason who's re-potting and he thinks it'd be nice, in a way, if he could get geraniums into his play about C.S. Lewis and J.R.R. Tolkien.

'We don't want the Press at our wedding,' he says to Jason. 'Everyone's got to "keep mum"', he says.

'Are we going to have a honeymoon? Capri? Marrakesh?' Jason asks.

'Fuck off,' Brian says.

Brian doesn't do holidays. Jason knows that. Jason's not bothered. That's the thing about Jason, he doesn't get bothered. Apart from loving him, that's what Brian likes about him. He doesn't get into a bother.

'Where have all the years gone?' Brian asks. 'The years, Jason, they seem to go by quicker than they ever did,' he says.

Rachel and Peter are in the shop. It is eight o'clock and they're still open.

'Put on the *'Aretha Now'* album,' she says.

'I thought we were packing it in for the day,' Peter says.

'No,' she says, 'Put it on, Peter.'

So, Peter does and Aretha sings *'Think'* and then *'Say a Little Prayer'* and then *'See Saw'*, and Rachel and Peter sing along and dance. And customers, two girls, three young men, devotees, come in, and join the dance.

2014. Saturday evening. The square is empty of people. The plane trees have been pollarded. In 2002 the building where the nurses once lived was bought, along with the two adjoining houses, by an overseas company based in the Cayman Islands on behalf of a Russian businessman, who sold it on to a Saudi businessman. It has now lain empty for three years, apart from an intense period of five weeks when the squatters movement took possession of it with their posters Homes for the People. Four of the buildings, the big handsome Victorian properties across the square have been converted into luxury flats and single dwellings. Most of their owners this weekend are in the country or overseas. The corner shop is now a personal trainer's outlet.

From one of the houses, from the downstairs apartment, can be heard distantly the Persian song *'Mimiram Barat'*.

On a low wall, sheltered from the natural wearing down by time and the elements, in faded red paint, are the letters PET and after a space there's what looks like the letter R and further along the word LOVES can be made out and then the letters RACH and then a space and there's the letter L.

DROWNINGS

Mrs Jenkins, just on eighty, in her red brick terraced house beyond the station. Her husband dead after two years of decline, his mind and then his body gone. Hauled from home to hospital, back and forth, month after month, week after week, day after day until he had been settled in his final hours in the hospice side ward, as thin as a rake, as the neighbours said. Incoherent. Unintelligible. Mrs Jenkins, his wife of sixty years, had been, as she told her neighbour, at his side seven days a week, every week, every month of the two long grievous years of his dying.

Him gone these past four months, Mrs Jenkins was now full to the tip of her nose with anger, guilt, exhaustion, an inability to remember the time of day, only her now with her cat in the bed. Her son had said 'Move on'. 'Move on,' he had said to her on the telephone from Los Angeles where he worked. She could not remember what it was he did. 'You've got to move on,' he said. 'Get out, keep active, take up again what you used to enjoy,' he said. 'Of course,' she said.

But after his call, she could not for the life of her remember what it was he had said or whether it had been today or yesterday he had telephoned. Yes, she told him, told herself, she would take up again what it was she used to enjoy. She told herself she would.

But it had been two years. 'Don't leave it too long,' her son had said on the telephone. 'I've got to go and feed the cat,' she had said. Would that not suffice? Had she not endured? Was she to blame? Did she not do her duty by her husband?

Barry Larkin, in his late seventies, on his fifth pint in The Belvedere Arms, lost his second wife six months earlier. Talking with friends, proclaiming his motto for life as, for him, it had become. Making known his practised remedy, the way, he pronounced confidently, of dealing – yes, dealing was the word – with grief. 'Keep active,' he said. 'Don't let the grass grow,' he said. 'Get out and about. That's what she would want,' he said to all and sundry, to those who bothered to listen to him, for they had heard it all before. They did not doubt they'd hear it all again, for that was old Barry since his second wife passed on, him sitting at the round hard wood table by the bar from opening to closing. All very jolly. All very certain of his declared conviction that the best thing when it came to loss, so to speak, gents, to grief, ladies and gents, was to keep active. 'You're right there,' one or another would say, which pleased old Barry no end. He knew how to keep his head above water. He knew how to hold off the feelings, feelings to which he could not put a name or understand, feelings best left alone, put aside. 'Keep active,' he said as he drowned himself in his tenth pint of the landlord's very best.

DUNCAN

Duncan was in his library which was very narrow by conventional standards. In it was his desk at which he was sitting, and there were bookshelves from floor to ceiling on the wall behind him, and again on either side of the marble fireplace. Before retirement Duncan had been a senior manager with a Life Assurance Company in the City. Daphne, his wife of forty years, was seated in the drawing room. He could see her through the open door. She was seated in an armchair below one of the two tall windows facing the garden at the back of the house. She was writing a letter. She was an enthusiastic letter writer. This was a peaceful place, a house of order, of some quiet luxury. The house was in Fulham. Daphne was writing a letter to her young lover, whom he had never met.

Duncan knew he had seen them together. He had ascertained they met regularly every Wednesday in Marples the coffee shop in Barrack Street. Then the two of them would go off, take a taxi, to his place he assumed. Or a seedy hotel. Did he mind? Not really. Well, if it was sex she was after, then he couldn't in fairness complain. His wife and he didn't indulge in that neck of the woods. Fact was he couldn't manage it anymore anyway. And the passion, the urge had more or less gone. No, if it was just sex, well, good luck to her. We all have our needs. But it was her writing letters to him in their house he didn't like, not one bit. He had purchased this house on his retirement three years earlier. It had been his money, his pension that paid for it. It was his money that had paid for pretty well everything over the years. She had worked now and then of course, this job and that, temporary work, but one couldn't say she had provided much in the way of finance from which to contribute to their present standard of living. No. He objected to the letters. If she had to write letters to him, whoever he was, she could go and do so in the library, or in the park if it was a fine day, somewhere or other, but not in his house. The trouble was, of course, how to approach her, how to bring about this change? The fact is, he told himself, she doesn't know I know she has a lover. Or at least he didn't think she knew he knew. And if he told her not to write to her lover in the house, she'd know he knew and that would lead to a scene, and one of the things he couldn't abide, more than her writing letters in the house to her lover, was a scene. He couldn't abide a squabble of any sort or, when it came down to it, even arguments. He liked, valued the quiet life. So, he was in a quandary.

Duncan got up and poured himself a scotch, although it was only just after twelve noon. His son John had been away for three years. He hadn't known this house. Duncan thought of his son John as being 'lost'. He knew where he was. He was in Manchester. But he had never visited them since he left London. He had written to him and his mother, (especially to his mother), once a fortnight at first, but after that, once every two months, and then, this past year, he hadn't written at all. He was 'lost'. Come to think of it, he said to himself, Daphne's mind being everywhere and anywhere other than where she was, she too could be declared 'lost'. Thank God, he thought, he had his books. He liked books. He liked looking at the covers as much as reading them. He had found that these last couple of years, since retiring, he could take a book from the shelves and just look at it, at the dust cover, at the binding. Reading it had become more of an effort. Daphne liked books too. She read in bed before turning out the light and in the mornings as she drank her coffee. When she wasn't reading, she was writing her letters to her lover. He went over to the shelves with a large scotch, and at random took down a book, took it over to his desk, sat down, and gazed at its cover.

Duncan liked walking. He did a lot of walking. He'd walk down the road to the shops and back again. He'd take the long way and make it over to the park. He liked the park. There were people in the park. People with dogs. He didn't like dogs, didn't trust dogs. There were people, young mothers or nannies, with small children walking with them or in the push chairs. He never spoke to them or even smiled, as that, he felt, could be misconstrued. He'd heard of a man, a botanist, who had taken his young son into the bushes to have a look at some insect or other and the police came up and took him in for questioning. Must have been a shock to him and to the child. And one knows what the general public is like: the 'no smoke without fire' mentality. A colleague of his told of a chap who went walking in the park, came across a young girl about five, in tears, on her own. Very cautious he was, his colleague told Duncan. The fellow put his hands behind his back, bent towards the girl, asked if she'd lost her mummy, whereupon this brute of a woman with tattoos all across her bosom had emerged from the trees, went off at high pitch accusing him of being a paedophile, quite dreadful. The poor man apparently had gone home in a terrible state, hadn't come outside for a week. That's the sort of thing that could happen. One had to be so careful. Duncan didn't go to the pub. He'd thought of doing so. He'd thought it would be rather pleasant, good for one, to get out and pop into a local, sit with a pint, chat with the regulars. But he didn't like beer. Not that much. And that was what chaps in a pub drank. Whisky would seem out of place, he felt. It would seem odd. Alien. And, anyway, how long would it take him to drink a pint, and he couldn't drink more than one. He hadn't the stomach for it. Also, he was concerned that, when he got chatting to others in there, other men, one or more of them might insist on buying him a beer, buying a round, and then he would have to buy them a beer and himself a beer and that wouldn't agree with him at all. So, he didn't go to the pub. This, he reckoned, was a pity, as it might have been what he needed, to get out and talk to people and spend time in company, while Daphne at home read her books and wrote her letters to her lover, and the boy got on with his life up in Manchester, which, he imagined, was much more satisfying than his own.

He went over to the shelves again, took down another book, took it over to his desk, sat down, and gazed at its cover.

At that moment, Daphne came in.

'I've had a letter. From our son John,' she said.

'Ah. Good show. What's the news?'

'He's getting married.'

'Is he? Gosh. Who to?'

'He doesn't say.'

'Oh.'

'A girl in Manchester, one supposes.'

'I see. When is the happy event?'

'He doesn't say.'

'Mm. Well, perhaps he'll write and tell us, and invite us to the wedding.'

It was difficult for him to say how many weeks it was before he broached the subject of their son with Daphne again. It was a Monday. He was at his desk. She was passing by his open door on her way, he assumed, to the kitchen with her coffee cup.

'Have you heard from him?' he asked.

'Who?' she asked.

'The boy.'

'What – what boy?'

'You know – for goodness sake – our son.'

'Oh, him. Yes. No. No, I haven't.'

'Had hoped he'd tell us when the wedding is.'

'Oh, yes. He's had that. He and the girl got married three weeks ago. I had a letter from him.'

'Oh. I didn't know.'

'I forgot to show it to you. Slipped my mind, dear.'

'Right. Anything else? In the letter?'

'No. Just that they're married and they're emigrating to Australia.'

'Emigrating? Australia? When?'

'He didn't say.'

'You'd think he'd tell us.'

She shrugged.

One morning sometime later he remembered his son, married now and planning to emigrate. He tracked Daphne to the garden where she was pruning a rose bush.

'No word?' he asked Daphne.

'About what?'

'The boy, he and his wife emigrating, when they're off.'

'Oh, yes. They've gone. They're there. He wrote. I forgot to tell you. My mind was on other things, elsewhere. They're in Melbourne.'

'What are they doing in Melbourne?'

'Well, at this time of the day, in Melbourne, it would be night, so I imagine they're asleep, or making love, or whatever these young people do.'

He returned to his study and poured himself a scotch, although it was only just after twelve noon. He took a book from the shelves, but couldn't read the title. He went to sip his whisky but couldn't seem to discover the glass which he thought had been in his hand. He decided it was best if he just remained quiet, and waited. And when he felt better and more like it, he'd pop out to the pub, have a chat with the regulars, buy a round, pop over and see the boy and his wife in Melbourne. He'd report into the office, get some work done, meet this girl, Daphne, young thing, in her twenties, bit of a beauty, nice clothes, fair hair, propose, see the boy, pick him up, play footer with him in the park, when he was better, felt more like it.

IN THE LONG GRASS

'Come quickly,' Annie said holding out her hand.

They stood at the top of Marsham cornfield, its crop newly cut to stubble, down towards his boyhood woods.

'Come on, Bernard,' she called as she hauled him forward and down and down until they reached the woods outer edge, and then on to the pasture beyond the narrow smelly brook and into the long grass.

She on her back, he at her side, all love and lusting, and she an angel with a pair of legs to kill for, with his hand on her knee and 'No further up, thank you. I'll have to know you better before you touch me there.'

He touches her lips with his and she unbuttons the top of his shirt, no more than that. Not yet, not today.

'I've got to get back for tea,' she said. 'They're expecting me.'

So, heave-ho, up they go, she on her long legs, he a little paunchy and only thirteen years of age.

'Come on,' she said, her hand in his, leading the way to propriety, through the wood, up the stubbled corn field and onto the roadway.

She turns to him with that smile and a laugh.

'See you,' she says and walks away towards her parent's house in the street at the end of the world.

He couldn't pass a day without wanting to see her face, to touch that knee, to lie there with her among the long grass.

'Come on, dizzy head,' his mother called as he stood at her kitchen door. 'Tea's ready,' she said. 'Where have you been? You been fighting in the woods with those boys from Corkstone Street? Dear God, look at you. What would your father say?'

His father worked for the Post Office and said nothing.

'He'll find his own way,' he had once said when asked how he thought the boy was doing.

Annie with the legs went off with Jamie and then with Pete and didn't as much as look at Bernard who lay alone in the grass beyond the woods at the bottom of the stubby field. And for a time, what seemed a long time, it was just Bernard and Bernard in the dark nights until later – he sixteen – there was Jean who removed her white T-shirt, lifted it above her head and so exposed her breasts and fulsome they were. She had earlier removed his hand as he had eagerly sought the tops of her thighs, and here in recompense she, at the end of her parent's vegetable garden, lifted her T-shirt. And he looked and didn't know what next to do.

ELLEN

There we are, seven o'clock Tuesday morning it is, outside Merseyside District cleaning depot. 'Our young ladies' as supervisor Alec calls us. Street cleaners we are. Togged out, drab green rain-proof overalls, buttoned up to the neck. Wide, utility caps.

It's Tuesday, seven o'clock. Young Florrie was wed to Arthur, married yesterday afternoon, they were, 10th of May 1915, at St Barnabas, Mossley Hill. Arthur is on shore leave. He'll be back at sea soon, fighting the Germans. You'll not know, day to day, from hour to hour, what's going to happen, the torpedoes, our ships going down. You can't be sure, but one has to hold on, hold to the day as it is, us women out there now, in Liverpool, North and South, out and about doing the men's work, them away at war with the Germans, on land and sea.

Florrie's the heroine, the special one, this morning, for last night was her first night with husband Arthur and they did it, he did it.

'Was it, you know?' I asked Florrie this morning, outside the Merseyside District cleaning depot, waiting with the others, with Brigid, Betty, Frances and Maeve, for supervisor Alec to get off his arse, to turn up with his rota for the morning shift.

I asked her and Florrie smiled. The smile she has on her lips,

117

the smile in her hazel eyes. It was all right then, it was. He did the right thing by her.

The men at war, dead and alive. Women on the Home Front, doing the work the men do. God knows, someone has to clean the streets, deliver the coal, work in armaments up there in Bootle. There's me now, with a husband Tomas with a broken back from a fall working down at Albert Dock. It was a rough and ready occasion it was with Tomas the first night we got married, for the poor man had no finesse in the matter, no degree of understanding of my part in the whole enterprise. Only, he gets better at it once he's lost the nerves, and soon enough there's the kids, one a year for six years. Then the man has enough of the business, and so has I, and thank God for that, for I'd not have lasted out with another child, the doctor said, had not needed to say. I knew it myself, I did.

RMS Lusitania gone down on the Friday. Friday the 7th of May 1915. It'll not be forgotten, not in Liverpool. Not by the men and women of Merseyside.

Brigid, standing in the line outside the cleaning depot, her husband among the crew. Best keep busy, her family say. That's the way it's done. At the bottom of the sea, Brigid's husband along with all of the others, at the bottom of the sea they lie, at the bottom of the sea Brigid's husband Cormac, the postman Finbar, named after Saint Finbar of Cork, his mother used to say, Finbar's boy, him too. Bound for home, for Liverpool, for the Prince's Landing Stage that afternoon, they say. On the Friday, torpedoed by the German U Boat, sunk beneath the waves off the Southern coast of Ireland. Best keep busy, Brigid, they say. Brigid thirty-five, looking fifty, and is it no wonder?

Brigid, me, Florrie, Frances, Maeve and Betty, waiting for Alec to get his arse over with the morning's rota, with news of another street with the window glass and debris all over the roadways.

Betty, plump unmarried Betty, in her forties, does it by herself, they say. Sweet smiling Betty. Never had a man touch her there, and never touched a man there and seems no worse for it.

Frances, funny dotty Frances. She's not saying, but it's understood she one time walked out with a Chinaman on his shore leave.

And Maeve. Maeve with us there now with her red hair, and with her husband, *her* husband too, God help us, her husband Ned in RMS Lusitania at the bottom of the Atlantic Ocean, with 1,198 passengers and crew, 750 tons of ammunition and artillery shells, it is said. 1,198 souls, Irish, American, English among them and eighteen minutes it took for the ocean liner to go down, go down with Brigid's husband Cormac and Maeve's Ned, along with 1,198 passengers and crew. Maeve with red hair, red-rimmed eyes long dried out with weeping. Maeve at one time fancied by the pork butcher's son in Robson Street, but a butcher's wife was never not one for Maeve. There's only her poor young Ned on the Atlantic bed, his face, his head between her small white as white breasts, the memory of his soft boyish eyes, his sweet smile lying deep in her heart, in the bosom of the sea. He and 1,198 others, of which 696 were crew.

It's seven o'clock, Tuesday morning. The sun rising above the Mersey, above the Irish Sea. There's a chill in the air. There's war abroad. War at home, my God. The Lusitania riots they'll be called, they will. All Saturday, Sunday, Monday, from north of the city, Scotland Road near the docks, Stanley Road, Linacre Road and beyond. Men, boys, women, raging through the streets, attacking the German Pork Butchers' on County Road, in Robson Street, Mr Fischer's on Walton Lane. Shops ransacked, windows shattered, belongings, beds, tables, chairs, tin baths out of windows into the street, smashed up they have been. The Dimler family, their grand Sea View House in Litherland Park looted, well-nigh demolished – the German Dimler family, pork butchers' shops in Liverpool and Bootle, and there's their two sons with the British army fighting the Germans.

Alec's 'little entourage', as he speaks of us women, are out and about in Fox Street, Mile End, first thing, sweeping up the mess.

'It's not the rioters, the hooligans, the screaming men and boys and women of North and South Liverpool, the mindless turnips,' I say to Florrie in Price Street, the two of us wading through the debris. 'Not them who have done all this, who are raising a finger to clear up their mess, no. And Mr Swarb, his shop smashed up too on account of his German wife and God knows how many years the Swarbs have lived in Birkenhead, off Price Street. It's a disgrace.'

'The Swarbs a decent family,' I tell my Tomas, him come in the kitchen from lying down on his back in the bedroom. 'A good honest family,' I tell him, putting out his tea. 'The ugly angry mob smash up Charles Dashley's butcher's shops in Price Street and Oxton Road, the rooms above not a thing standing. Charles Dashley himself, I hear, kicked in the head. It's a disgrace. Isn't it enough we're fighting the Germans from Germany itself, the real Germans, their torpedoes, their ships and all, and us turning on our own as we seem to be?' I say. For I'm tired and tired of it all, I tell him.

'Is your tea all right? Is it to your liking?' I say.

'It is,' he says.

The kids are outside and off my hands, Brendan, Donal and Josh with Josh's football, Fiona with her friend Claire over at Claire's mother's. Gerry, the eldest, is helping out at the Grunter's hardware, his after-school job and thank God for that.

It's Wednesday afternoon, the morning street-cleaning shift over and done with, I'm off through the rain to clean for Mrs James in Winterhill Close, her front steps, the kitchen floor, the dusting. Mrs James a pleasant enough woman with her husband in taxation, a professional gentleman. Mrs James this afternoon on about the riots, the damage done, the dreadful behaviour, the Catholics and Protestants, the North and South Liverpool, at each other's throats as ever was.

'So much hate between them and to what purpose, do they not worship the same God?' Mrs James says, standing over me, me on my hands and knees, giving her kitchen floor a thorough doing over, doing the job proper. She'll have no cause to complain. 'Have we not enough with the Germans,' she says, 'with our men out there in France, at sea fighting for their lives, for God's sake, these Catholics, these Protestants, these hooligans fighting and abusing each other?'

'And thank you, Ellen,' she says to me. 'The floor, it looks very well, it's made a difference. Have I paid you yet? It's on the side table. And you and your husband with his back, the poor man,' she says.

I'm down her front path, her words hanging in my ears. I'm in the street on my way to old Mrs Cuthbertson, I hear Mrs James call goodbye now and her closing her front door.

It's Thursday, seven o'clock, waiting for Alec outside the depot, and there he is now. The man is not at sea, fighting in France, not working the docks, not like my Tomas before his accident, before he broke his back down at Albert Dock. Not Alec, on account of his heart, the doctors said. No sign of Brigid.

'Brigid's in the kitchen,' her mother says to me.

I call in after morning shift.

'Been in the kitchen all day now,' her mother says.

Sitting there, she's been, not a word, not a thing to eat, just sits. It's taken her of a sudden, her Cormac drowned with the rest. It's hit her sudden.

'Her Cormac's brother Michael was out with them again last night, ransacking the Germans,' her mother says. 'Although they say it's anybody foreign now, Italian, Spanish, Dutch. Cormac's brother Michael, bereft he is, full of anger, raging he is against his brother's death. The man was purple in the face,' Brigid's mother tells me. 'When he popped in last night and again first thing this morning, by the looks of him, ready to kill he was.'

'How are you?' I say to Brigid.

There's nothing to say, it's all there in her face, in her sitting, not moving. 'It's trauma,' I say.

'Is that bad?' Brigid's mother asks.

'You ought to get the doctor,' I say.

'So I will,' Brigid's mother says. 'I'll go down there now while you're with her.'

She puts on her coat, leaves the house. I sit with Brigid and wait.

'I'll make a cup of tea,' I say.

It's half through the afternoon and I ought to be at Mrs Williams on South Road, her kitchen floor, the dusting, in less than twenty minutes, but I have to wait till Brigid's mother returns, and there she is, all out of breath and in a hurry.

'The doctor says he'll come later when he has a moment,' she says.

'I best be off,' I say. 'I've got Mrs Williams, South Road.'

'Ah, that's fine,' says Brigid's mother. 'And thank you, coming along, seeing how she is, and the doctor will be here soon.'

Betty is at St Mary of Angels in Fox Street for the remembrance service for those lost on RMS Lusitania. That's where she goes. Like a magnet it is to her, St Mary of Angels in Fox Street. The way she talks of it. There's Father Richards there, a fine young man appointed to the church since it opened only five years ago and isn't it a lovely place of worship, Betty tells me she says to the woman next to her. Designed by Pugin and Pugin itself with its fine marble interior and Italian High Renaissance fixtures, as she has been told, told by Father Richards himself who is as proud as can be, being parish priest of St Mary of Angels in Fox Street, and today it's packed full to the walls, to the doors, without a doubt, and no wonder, it being a terrible blow to the community as it is. Betty, from County Wicklow, her voice in my head. Betty herself now looking out for Father Richards himself after the service of remembrance, seeking as she is a few words, a few words only, no matter what may be said, a passing word or two with the man. For has she not discovered in herself that after a word or two with Father Richards she feels better in herself and with the world and her loneliness, she not having married and with no mother and father worth speaking of her own, the mother being gone since Betty was six and her father no father to her with his drinking and swearing and disregard and no help in any way in the matters of her life or anyone's for that matter. No, she is alone, she knows it, has to endure it, but two or three words it takes from Father Richards and she feels a lot, lot better for them. For Father Richards is a holy man devoted to God's work and to his impoverished congregation, his people in North Liverpool. He is a man who himself would always remain unmarried, wifeless as Betty thinks of it, and him so young and strong looking and with no wife to share his bed. God help her, she mustn't think like this, not about bed, bed and Father Richards, it's a sin, she thinks. A sin to do so, so it is, but there it is, the man, with no wife, no children of his own, and they say a man without sexual outlet is a man to beware, unless of course, they say, the man is a priest, because somehow or other, Betty has heard it said, a priest is blessed by God in such a way so as not to have the sexual need to the extent the ordinary man in his congregation has. So there we are, Betty O'Brien, now you know, but it is a puzzle for all that, and something strange and beyond comprehension, which is how it ought to be, for no ordinary human being can be expected to understand the workings of the Almighty, Betty O' Brien, not how it is that the good Lord Above allowed RMS Lusitania to go under as she did.

'And was it possible, Father Richards,' she had asked him, 'that the Lord Himself is on the side of the Germans as much as He is on the side of Liverpool?'

When she asked him that, he said, 'There are good folk in all lands and in all races, Betty, one cannot deny it. It is the governments,' he said. 'The people are led by good and evil,'

And Father Richards' words lay on her a calming effect, such was his conviction and the steady timbre of his speaking.

Seven o'clock the Friday morning, Alec on time for once outside the depot with his jobs-to-do. In attendance Florrie, me, Betty and Frances, Maeve with her red hair, her eyes red-ringed. Brigid is at home, sitting in the kitchen. Her husband Comack deep under water, asleep on the ocean bed. Beyond speech, she is.

THE STORIES PUBLISHED IN THE COLLECTION

Store Security won second prize in the 2019 Wells Festival of Literature Short Story Competition. 2019

Sarah was short-listed for the Bridport Short Story Prize 2019, and long-listed for the V.S. Pritchett Short Story Prize 2018. It was published by Hammond House Publishing in the anthology *Leaving* in 2020.

'Our Revels Now Are Ended' was long listed for the Dorset Fiction Award 2018.

From Across The Sea was longlisted for the Exeter Writers Prize 2020.

City Walk (edited version) published in *Write Time Anthology One* in 2019.

Carmil Forester was published in *Valve Journal* (Glasgow) 2015

The Square and *Ellen* were published in the anthology *'Eavesdropping'* (BSWG).

Duncan was published in *The Irish Literary Review* 2015.

ABOUT THE AUTHOR

Christopher Owen's stories have been published in a number of literary magazines and anthologies in the UK, USA and Ireland. He has won second prize in the Wells Festival of Literature Short Story Competition.

He has been shortlisted for the Bridport Story Prize and for the Hammond House Publishing Prize.

He's been long-listed for the Royal Society of Literature V. S. Pritchett Short Story Prize 2018, the Dorset Short Story Prize and for the London Short Story Prize 2018.

His plays have been produced in the UK, Ireland, USA, Australia and the Gulf States. His plays have been long-listed for the Papatango New Writing Prize and by the Bush Theatre, London. In the 1990s he toured the UK and Gulf States with his one man show *A Parson's Tale*.

An actor for many years, he has worked extensively in theatre, television and film. He lives in London with his family.